THE MIDNIGHT GHOSTS

Emma Fischel

Illustrated by
Adrienne Kern

Contents

The Letter

A nt and Sally read through the letter with some trepidation. There was no getting out of it now. They really were going to stay at Twelve Bells End. It was a pity they couldn't remember more about the house or cousin Max. But everything they had heard led them to think that this could be a very strange week.

"You never know, it might be fun," said Ant uncertainly . . .

Ant   Sally

Twelve Bells End,
Gloomwood Road,
Middle-Knight-on-Sea.

November 6th

Dearest Sally and Anthony,

Isn't this a dreary time of year? Your uncle Manley and I simply *must* escape to Mythika for a week's sun. Thrilled you can pay our precious son Max a visit while we are away. He does so need company of his own age. How tiny you were when we last saw you! Do you remember how Max cut up your skipping rope and fed it to you, saying it was spaghetti — such high spirits!
   You'll find us a full household. People visit and, somehow, never leave. We seem to have had some unfortunate accidents over the years, though. And, strangely, all at midnight too! (Dear Manley was never the same after the accident with the cheese grater seven years ago this week, and — between ourselves — the others are not much better. Then there's the professor. Hardly had he arrived (just over a couple of years ago now and without two pennies to rub together) than, overnight, he almost completely lost his hearing.)
   Our fortunes seem to have taken a downward turn these last two years. I'm afraid the house is a trifle shabby. (Mrs Mopps, of course, has been an absolute treasure since she arrived in June — although one could wish for just a *shade* more enthusiasm for the dusting.) Too bad there seems to be no one to take over the title and restore the house to fortune! It's nearly fifty years now since Melrose passed away. And where is Magnus? So sad Magnolia took him away when he was so small (rumour has it that he was seen three years ago on Saddlesore racecourse, gambling away his fortune).

Well, darlings, we'll expect you on the eleventh. All love, your auntie Crystal xxx

PS I dug out a few photos for you. The one of my sister Posy was taken on the night of her tragic fall. The happy couple are your great-aunt Myrtle and great-uncle Harvey.

Manley, me and darling Max

POSY
12th NOV

Outside the family villa

The Journey

A ll along the platform the last stragglers were slamming doors shut behind them. Ant and Sally leapt on to the train, gasping. The guard blew the whistle and the train pulled slowly out of the station.

Sally barged her way through the carriage in search of an empty window seat. Ant followed her, red-faced and puffing under the weight of most of their luggage. Sally settled herself comfortably in the seat facing forwards while Ant collapsed in a heap opposite her.

Sally started to feel more hopeful now that they were on their way. Staying in a grand old house might have its compensations and, after all, cousin Max would have grown up by now. Ant, too, began to ponder the possibilities. Meanwhile, Sloth the cat slumbered peacefully, dreaming only of a warm fire and the smell of fresh fish.

The train started to gather speed. The journey ahead was a long one. Ant and Sally sat back and stared out of the window, both lost in thought. What would the coming week hold in store?

After half an hour Sally got out some tapes. She was soon humming along to Peter Out and the Fadeaways. She played her entire collection twice, then tuned in to the radio. She learned some useful facts about ornamental hedge-clipping before switching off.

Ant whiled away the time with snacks from the buffet car. Then he practised a new card trick. After that, he counted fence posts flashing past the window. At 142, he gave up.

The journey became more and more boring. Only Sloth, snoring contentedly, seemed to be enjoying it. Station after station flashed past. Grime-caked chimneys gave way to thick, dark forests, then to bleak moorlands. Still the train rushed on, ever deeper into the countryside . . .

With a sudden jolt the train shuddered to a halt, the brakes screeching on the tracks. Ant and Sally woke with a start. The carriage was empty. They were the only passengers left on the train. They shivered in the icy air. It seemed to be much colder. Outside, the station name loomed out of the fog. This was it – the end of the line.

They stumbled onto the dark platform. The place was deserted. No ticket collector, no telephone, nothing but a single flickering light by the exit. They looked around uneasily as they waited . . . and waited.

A Twist of Fate

The fog swirled around them in chilly whorls, while the icy night air knifed through their clothes. Whichever way they looked, the road disappeared into inky blackness.

Suddenly, a shape loomed from the distant shadows. "Yoohoo!" Sally called, but her voice was lost in the rustling of tree branches blown and buffeted in a sudden angry breeze.

Was it imagination or did the shadowy stranger seem to beckon them to follow him?

Sinister shadows darted and flickered across their path as Ant and Sally chased after the caped figure. Moonlight glimmered through gaps in the scudding clouds. Tree branches clawed at the sky like bony fingers, while all around them they could hear faint rustling sounds from the undergrowth. Something swooped overhead – an owl scouring the ground in search of night-time prey, his yellow eyes glinting in anticipation.

Ant yelled and Sally shouted as they ran, but the fleeing shadow never stopped – or spoke. Then, gasping for breath, they rounded a corner and skidded to a halt. "He's gone," said Sally, in bewilderment, "Vanished!"

Ant didn't reply. He had spotted a battered old sign, half-hidden under a tangle of weeds. Crouching down, he wiped at its grimy surface with his sleeve. "Look," he said, staring at the shabby, peeling paintwork, "Gloomwood Road!"

Sally gasped with relief. By some strange twist of fate the caped stranger had led them to exactly where they wanted to be . . .

They fought their way along the weed-choked, unlit lane. At last they came to an imposing pillared gateway. Beyond it curved a long driveway. "This is it," said Sally, "Twelve Bells End!"

Daunted, they stared. Towering above them, stretching high into the moonlit sky, was the dark and forbidding outline of an enormous house. Old and neglected, only the occasional flickering light at a window showed that someone lived there . . .

Journey's End

Sally lifted the heavy brass knocker on the front door. It hit the ancient wood with a loud, dull thud. There was a long pause, followed by the faint sound of approaching footsteps.

Stomachs churning, Ant and Sally watched the door handle begin to turn. Then a face poked slowly round the door frame.

"Ha-ha-hallo," stuttered Sally. "W-w-w-we've come to stay. We g-g-got a letter . . . "

And then a second face popped out. At least this one looked jollier. "Hello!" it said, beaming. "You must be Sally and Anthony!"

The door opened wide and the owner of the face came forward with outstretched hands. "Pleased to meet you," he said, pumping Sally's arm up and down. "I'm Maximilian."

So *this* was their cousin Max. It was good to see a friendly face after that long dark walk.

Max turned to the frowning woman. "And this is Mrs Mopps, the housekeeper," he said. "Mrs Mopps, meet my cousins. They've come to stay."

"Will they be here long?" the housekeeper asked sourly, pursing her lips into a tight, straight line.

"About a week," answered Max. He beckoned to Ant and Sally to follow him inside the dark and uninviting house.

Ant and Sally hovered on the step then, gingerly, they stepped inside. The door clanged shut behind them.

They were in a narrow, musty corridor, dimly lit by dripping candles burning in ornate holders. Ahead, the sinister housekeeper slipped swiftly and silently away through the flickering shadows.

Nervously, they followed Max. What lay in store beyond the dark-panelled corridor?

"This is the main hallway," Max announced as they emerged from the dark and musty corridor. Stupefied, Ant and Sally stared around. Did people really live here? The place looked more like a museum than a house. It was a jumble of dusty portraits, ancient carvings, marble busts . . . And could that old man studying the globe really be one of their relatives?

Max hurried them towards a winding flight of stairs. Somewhere, far away in the house, a clock began to strike the hour. Sally shivered. It was colder inside this strange old house than it had been outside in the fog.

9

Surprises in Store

The ancient floorboards creaked and groaned under their feet as they climbed slowly up the stairs after Max. Outside, the wind moaned and sighed round the strange old house. The first drops of rain began to spatter against a cracked stained-glass window set deep into the wall.

At the top of the stairs, Sally clutched at the heavy wooden bannister. She gasped in disbelief. In front of her was a stout man on a unicycle. To her amazement, Max didn't seem to be surprised. "That's Mervin," he whispered to Ant and Sally, as the unicyclist sped past them and bumped his way down the stairs, "Your second cousin, twice removed."

Abruptly, Max turned left into a maze of dark, gloomy corridors, faintly lit by guttering candles. He led Ant and Sally through a huge stone archway into a vast gallery. "Here's the family!" he said.

From floor to ceiling, from centuries past to the present day, the entire Midnight family stared down at them. Before Ant and Sally could do more than glance around, Max hurried them on. But it seemed as if the eyes in every portrait swivelled and turned to follow them . . .

They went up some narrow, wooden stairs, then right along a corridor. At last Max stopped outside a gnarled oak door. He turned the handle. The door swung open. "Hope you like the room," said Max, disappearing.

With thudding hearts, Ant and Sally stepped inside. What more strange sights would this ancient and mysterious house reveal?

Shadows flickered in every corner. Outside, thunder grumbled angrily in the distance. A flash of lightning lit up the two chairs by the fire. Inside the house, a clock began to strike loudly. Ant looked at his watch: seven o'clock. Surely the clock had struck more than that?

CLANG! They spun round. The window was swinging wildly backwards and forwards, the glass rattling in the frame. WHOOSH! A blast of icy air swirled round the room. Then the window slammed shut again. The wind died away and the room became still.

The air felt strangely calm . . . until, from above the fireplace, came a faint rustling noise. Meanwhile, from far away, the booming sound of a gong reverberated through the house. The rustling noise grew gradually louder. Ant and Sally stood, rooted to the spot. One by one, page after page was tearing off the calendar and spinning dizzily round the room.

11

Dinner is Served . . .

With mounting trepidation Ant and Sally made their way downstairs. The sound of babbling voices led them to the dining room. Nervously, they pushed the door open and went inside.

Gaping they stared around. Then Max ushered them towards two empty chairs. And so began the strangest evening of their lives. All they could do was watch and listen . . .

SOME VERY PECULIAR PEOPLE INDEED WERE SCRUTINIZING THEM IN STONY SILENCE.

AND THEN THE MEAL ARRIVED.

13

Mysterious Messages

At last, Ant and Sally made their escape. Back in their room, they shut the door with relief. Max had promised an action-packed schedule for the following day but, for the moment at least, they were alone.

"What a place," said Ant, "And what a meal!"

"What on earth is going on?" said Sally, slumping into a chair. "And why is everyone so strange?"

Ant decided to tackle the most pressing problem. Fortunately, he had emergency rations at hand. He tore the wrapping off a packet of biscuits and they munched their way through it, then another . . . and then a third.

Outside the weather was worsening. The strengthening wind howled down the chimney and driving rain lashed viciously at the windows. With sinking hearts, they got ready for bed. But they were in for a shock. So far, nothing in that strange old house had been quite what they expected – and their room was no exception.

The old house creaked and groaned as the ancient timbers settled for the night. Moonlight threw flickering shadows on to the walls and floor. Ant and Sally shivered under the icy bedclothes. They heard the sound of feet padding stealthily along the corridor. Did the footsteps stop outside their door? It was hard to be sure . . . At last they drifted off into uneasy sleep.

Little did they know that, while they slept, strange forces were at work in the old house. When all was dark and quiet, somewhere, the clock struck midnight. Inside the room nothing stirred. Then, from the floor, came a faint rustling noise. The scattered calendar leaves started to gather together, then flew up the chimney, vanishing without a sound.

Sally stirred restlessly. Was a faint faraway voice whispering her name? "Sally, Sally, wake up!" the eerie voice seemed to say, over and over again.

Ant rolled over, half asleep, half awake. Was a cold, clammy hand really clutching and clawing at his shoulder, shaking him into consciousness?

Quivering with fear and wide awake, they both sat bolt upright. "W-what's happening?" said Ant, clutching the bedclothes tightly around him.

"I d-don't know," said Sally, staring wildly around the room. "But I don't think I like it."

CRASH! A notebook flew off the shelf and landed, open, on the floor. Sloth jumped off the bed, yeowling with terror. He stood over the book, hissing and spitting, back arched and fur bristling. Ant and Sally watched, horror-struck, as wavering lines slowly appeared on the empty page – lines that spelled out just one single word.

CRRRRK! The door to the wardrobe started to open. Groaning and complaining, it swung slowly outwards. Then a message started to appear on the mirror. With unsteady strokes, word after word started to form before their eyes. Quaking with fright they saw that the words spelled out a desperate warning. But what did it mean?

WOOOOOOAHH! A blast of icy wind swept round the room and swirled into the fireplace. It caught up a bundle of paper scrumpled in the grate. Flapping and billowing, the paper unfolded. Ant and Sally were too terrified to move or speak. In front of them were the faded pages of an ancient newspaper.

Trembling, Sally picked up the crumpled, yellowing paper and spread it out on the floor in front of her.

15

HAVOC HITS HISTORIC HOUSE!

Exposed: *the chilling secrets of Twelve Bells End —
house of horror!*

From our correspondent
BILLY VITTORNOT

THE LATEST in a series of freak accidents to hit residents of Twelve Bells End happened at midnight last night when a man was badly concussed by a jar of pickled onions.

The accident happened when his cycle was in collision with the back of a van carrying groceries for the Pricewar chain of supermarkets. The cycle was split in two by the accident and the man was rushed to the casualty department of Gallstone General Hospital.

The man, a bachelor (43), was later named as Mervin Midnight of Twelve Bells End. He is said to be stable and asking for his bicycle.

Dogged by misfortune

THIS IS NOT the first time tragedy has hit Twelve Bells End. In a chain of bizarre coincidences many residents have suffered accidents resulting in personality changes and memory loss.

Victims of fate

ATTRACTIVE brunette Posy Tutu (39), once principal soloist with the Bolshy Ballet, was dropped in mid pas-de-deux by her leading man. The incident happened during a production staged at Twelve Bells End. Since then, Miss Tutu has hung up her ballet shoes and is now a regular at the Middle-Knight Junior soccer try-outs.

Merry prankster Juster Chuckle was once well-known for his practical jokes and hilarious one-liners — until he nearly died laughing. One night, while telling his favourite joke, the young wag laughed himself breathless, then fainted. Upon recovery, Chuckle was so shaken by the incident that he vowed never to laugh again. To avoid an accidental rib-tickler, he now speaks sentences backwards only. He plans to become a mathematics teacher.

**LATEST VICTIM:
Mervin Midnight**

**SOCCER-CRAZY:
Posy Tutu**

**TEEN-SCREAM TURNED
TEACH: Chuckle**

Midnight mansion

TWELVE BELLS END has been in the Midnight family for generations. The house was designed by the first Lord Midnight who drew heavily on his travels abroad for inspiration.

Inferno

THIRTY years ago yesterday, the house narrowly escaped destruction in a fire

Fire drama mansion

which swept through part of the east wing. The only victim was the twelfth Lord Midnight, despite vain attempts to save him by plucky local man Frank Forthright.

Also on the scene was Fireman Slift. Slift commented: "Lord Midnight seemed to be delirious towards the end. His last words were: 'A custard mouse and door to swallow me'."

Local lore: house is jinxed

Our reporter **MAY KITTUP** *has been on the spot to gauge local reaction to this latest tragic event*

THE SLEEPY VILLAGE of Middle-Knight-on-Sea is buzzing with talk of the strange goings-on at Twelve Bells End.

It seems that many villagers have long held the belief that the house is under some kind of jinx. Yet there was a strange reluctance on the part of most of the villagers to talk. One local man finally consented to meet me – but insisted he remain anonymous. We met under a small shrub in the car park behind the Spectre and Stone public house. Mr X seemed shifty and ill-at-ease while we spoke.

Local councillor Polly Bellowes, a familiar figure around the village

Village of fear

"They say there's rooms in that house have been empty and locked for years," Mr X claimed, checking around him nervously. "And once a year," he added in a whisper, "They say a caped figure paces the corridors, moaning and wailing and wringing his hands." With this, Mr X refused to say more and left.

Lone voice

ONE VILLAGER who doesn't share the general fears is Councillor Polly Bellowes. She scoffs at suggestions that the house might be cursed. "People round here," she commented, "Spend too much time in idle gossip." Following the latest accident, she has called for an enquiry into road maintenance policy.

My flaming battle!

Thirty years on, have-a-go hero Frank Forthright talks exclusively to the **SCORCHER** *about his bold rescue bid*

SHY FRANK, a confirmed bachelor (52), was unwilling to talk at first. "Why bring all that up? – it's history," commented the reluctant hero. He added, "I tried to save him – even he deserved a chance."

When asked if he could shed further light on Lord Midnight's last words, Mr Forthright became agitated and asked our reporter to leave. He declined to make any further comment.

REMEMBER!
You read it first in your
sizzling
SCORCHER!

Village of Fear

The next day dawned bright and sunny. Shafts of light beamed in through the old mullioned window in their room. Had the events of the night before ever really happened? It seemed hard to believe.

"I'm hungry," said Ant. "Let's go to the village." Sally agreed, glad to avoid another meal in the mysterious old house.

Quietly, they let themselves out of the front door and set off down the driveway.

At the end of Gloomwood Road they turned left. In the distance they could see clusters of houses huddled together, hugging the curves of the road as it twisted and turned on its way to the sea.

Walking towards the straggling outskirts of the village, an old woman stopped them. Slyly, she looked at Ant, then Sally.

"We don't like strangers here," she hissed. "You'd best be going." And with that, she scuttled away.

Taken aback, Ant and Sally walked slowly on. Ten minutes later they reached the village. But in the narrow high street they became uncomfortably aware of a great deal of attention . . .

The further into the village they went, the more the sensation grew. Heads swivelled. furtively to watch them. Prying eyes bored into their backs. Faces peered out from behind twitching curtains. But no one spoke a word to them – or almost no one.

Just then Ant felt an urgent tug at his sleeve. The anxious voice of an old man whispered in his ear. "You be the guests up at Twelve Bells End? Go! Leave while there's still time!" But before they could reply, he had fled.

Ant and Sally stared at each other. It hardly seemed possible. The entire village was scared to death . . . but why?

Nervously, they opened the door to the village store. The tinny bell rang out. Everyone inside the tiny shop turned to stare. Then there was silence.

"Here long?" the shopkeeper said at last.

"A week," Sally answered, to a sharp intake of breath from one of the customers.

"Are you sure that's wise?" asked the shopkeeper, heavily.

Ant hastily chose a packet of strawberry-flavoured Scrunchy-Munchies, then they paid up and left. But once they were outside the shop, they heard an urgent hissing noise behind them. They swivelled round . . .

PSSSST!

For a moment, Ant and Sally thought they were hearing things. But there was no doubt about it, someone lurking behind the wall was trying to attract their notice.

"There's someone you should meet – who knows more than he tells," whispered the anonymous voice. "Follow this road to the green, then look for the cottage with red windows. It's next to a blue cottage, on a slight hill. But hurry!"

Across the busy green they could see the house, just as the mystery voice had described it. They hesitated. What would lie in wait for them there?

The Story Unfolds . . .

Quaking slightly, Ant and Sally walked up the path to the cottage. Suddenly, there was a shout from the garden. Startled, they turned. A red-faced figure was approaching, brandishing his walking stick at them.

"Hullo. W-we're staying at T-Twelve Bells End," Sally babbled. The figure shuffled nearer. He seemed faintly familiar, somehow. Had they seen him somewhere before?

Then they recognized him. Advancing on them was a portlier, older version of heroic Frank Forthright from the newspaper. So *this* was who they had been sent to meet! But why?

Frank stared at them. He seemed agitated and about to speak, then changed his mind. He shuffled from foot to foot. At last he spoke. "Leave now," he said slowly. "No good will come of staying."

Then Ant butted in. "Please help us. There are strange things going on – things we can't explain," he said, "In the house, in the village . . . and our relatives . . . "

"Relatives?" interrupted Frank sharply. "You're members of the Midnight family?"

"Yes," said Ant, bewildered. "Why?"

Frank seemed deep in thought. Then, with a heavy sigh, he spoke. "You'd better come inside. There are things you need to know."

He beckoned Ant and Sally to follow him up the path. Inside the house, he led them to a small sitting room and gestured to three threadbare chairs ranged around the empty fireplace. "Sit down," he said, "And listen hard to what I have to say."

"Twelve Bells End is an evil place," he began. "It all started the night the fire broke out in the east wing many years ago . . . "

20

21

The Midnight Stone

There was a moment's silence as Frank's tale reached its chilling conclusion. Then Ant ventured, "The Stone? What Stone?"

Frank reached up to the bookshelf and took down a heavy old tome, covered with years of dust and grime.

The Midnight Stone

Property of the Midnight family, the Stone forms the centrepiece of a magnificent relic (pictured right). Intricately fashioned in pewter with rubies inset on the base, the relic has a matched pair of Loukaniki goats* ornately detailed on the upper surface. The Stone itself is made of cyanozine, one of the world's rarest minerals.

An artist's impression of the Midnight Stone and relic

Lord Midnight decreed that the Stone should forever stay within the Midnight family and never be sold

Origins of the Stone

The Stone came into the Midnight family after the first Lord Midnight, an intrepid explorer, discovered Mythika, a hitherto unknown country. Lord Midnight quickly became a favourite at the court of Queen Fatima (see opposite). A gifted linguist, he soon spoke fluent Mythikan, including seven regional dialects.

Alas, upon suggesting it was time for him to return to his native land, Queen Fatima clapped him in a dungeon. His only food was grilled lizards and pureed slugs, fed to him once a day through his prison bars.

The court jester, however, owed Lord Midnight a deep debt of gratitude. Some weeks earlier Lord Midnight had spoken eloquently in favour of a rise in basic wages for Fools. This had resulted in payment of an extra two olives per year for the jester.

When the jester overheard Fatima planning to execute Lord Midnight the following day, he plotted a daring jail break. The escape went as planned. As Lord Midnight prepared to flee the jester handed him the relic as a parting gift.

Lord Midnight bids farewell to the noble jester

Reproduction of a woodcut by Athos of Pathos

© *MOMMA (Museum of Medieval Mythikan Art)*

* Loukanikis are native only to Mythika. They are the country's national emblem.

"There," he said, jabbing a bony forefinger at the page they should read. "The Midnight Stone. Famed for its beauty and fated from the day it fell into the hands of the Midnight family!"

Ant and Sally were soon engrossed in the strange history of the ancient gem. Sloth, not such a keen historian, stalked off for a tour of the kitchen. When they finished reading, Frank closed the book, saying solemnly, "But that's not all. The story of the Stone doesn't end there!"

Historic Background to Stone

Lord Midnight, a keen diarist and amateur artist of some distinction, has left a source of valuable information about the Mythikan culture and people. Below are extracts from his jottings, with explanatory notes.

An excerpt from Lord Midnight's diary

She seemeth a goodlye sorte of monarche

the foole hath warned me not to lette it slippe into the wronge handes - for he sayeth it supporteth the moste strange and fantastik poweres.

1) Fatima (pictured above by Lord Midnight) is now widely regarded as one of the harshest Mythikan rulers. Mythikans were expected to perform continuous athletic feats, such as triple somersaults, back flips and handstands, while in her presence. Only those over ninety-five were exempt from this ruling.
2) For many centuries it was the duty of the jester to make up a new joke every hour. If the joke failed to make the ruling monarch laugh, the points on the jester's cap and shoes would be ceremonially snipped off with a pair of hedge clippers.

In addition, it was the traditional role of the jester to act as guardian of the relic. We have no record of what happened to the jester befriended by Lord Midnight.

A Family Scandal

Frank's eyes misted over as he started to recall the fateful events that followed in the history of the Stone. "It all took place one ordinary autumn afternoon," he began, "Two weeks before the fire that claimed the twelfth Lord Midnight . . ."

25

A Walk through the Woods

At last Frank concluded his mysterious tale. "That's all I can tell you," he said, slumping back in the shabby chair. "Now go. Take the short cut through the gate at the end of the road and go round the lake. But hurry!"

Ant and Sally stood up to go. Exhausted, Frank mopped at his brow with a large spotted handkerchief. "They say the one who finds the Stone can lift the curse," he continued weakly. "And that there's a secret room in the house that holds the key to the whereabouts of the Stone. Now leave me be – for it's rumoured that any who help those who meddle with the Midnight Stone may, too, fall foul of the curse!"

Ant and Sally hurried down the road, heads reeling. Could they really be staying in a house under the threat of an ancient curse? And who, they wondered uneasily, would the next victim be?

"How on earth do we find the Stone?" said Sally. "It's been missing for years."

Something about the story was niggling Ant. It was something the twelfth Lord Midnight had said when he cursed the house: "So long as the Stone is mine" . . . Why should he call the Stone *mine*, when his twin brother had stolen it? After all, the Stone had never been recovered.

Before Sally could reply, they reached the gate at the end of the road. Lifting the ancient latch, they pushed hard against the rotting wood. The hinges whined once in protest, then they were through.

Dense trees stretched above them, cutting out all but the faintest glimmer of sunshine. Half-blinded by the sudden change from light to shade, Ant and Sally hesitated a moment. Then, slowly, their eyes adjusted to the gloom . . .

What kind of place was this? Neglected for years, the stench of rot and decay was overpowering. No birds sang, no wind rustled the leaves, not a ripple disturbed the dank, dark water of the lake. Hearts pounding, Ant and Sally stumbled along the slippery bank. Branches scratched at their faces, brambles clutched at their feet, and then the path petered out. They were surrounded by an army of tall trees. It was impossible to tell which way to go. "We're lost," gulped Sally.

A cold, clammy feeling crawled up Ant's spine. A quiet voice had whispered his name, but there was no one in sight. Then, through the trees, Ant saw a dark, silent figure, beckoning them to follow him.

Ant and Sally struggled to keep up with the shadowy stranger who led them through the dark woods. His cape swirled round him as he moved. His feet seemed hardly to touch the ground as he glided silently onwards . . .

The Missing Window

Chinks of sunlight filtered through the trees. Ant and Sally could hear birds twittering in the distance. Then, blinking in the sudden light, they were out of the woods and on the edge of the garden. But there was no sign of the strange and shadowy figure who had led them from the lake. He had vanished as mysteriously as he had appeared.

They scanned the scene in front of them. The garden, still sodden from the heavy rain of the night, stretched away in front of them. In every corner they could see familiar faces from the meal of the evening before.

The morning sun glinted palely on the old house. The ancient stones had mellowed down the ages to a soft shade of grey. Sally peered at the first-floor windows and tried to work out which belonged to their room. The more she looked, the more something struck her as strange – but what was it?

Of course! Clutching Ant's arm, she spluttered, "Look! Next to our room. There was a window there once. Could there be a room behind it?"

They sprinted across the garden. Would they find a secret room? And could it hold a vital clue to the whereabouts of the Stone, as Frank had said?

They pounded up the steps, wrenched the back door open and thundered through the house. In frantic haste, they searched the length of the corridor outside their room. Surely there must be a door here somewhere?

Unknown to them, they were not alone in the dark and gloomy corridor. A lurking figure was watching every move they made and listening hard to every word they said . . .

Then Sally had a brainwave. Panting, they moved a heavy cabinet that was jutting out from the wall. Behind it, festooned in cobwebs, was a door!

Neither of them had heard the faint rustling of a starched skirt, nor noticed the sound of hurried footsteps disappearing round the corner . . .

Behind the Locked Door

With trembling hands, Sally grasped the key. It was almost jammed solid in the lock. At last, with a loud click, it turned. Ant pushed against the door. The age-old hinges, unoiled and unused for years, creaked into life.

It was like stepping into another world. Ant and Sally gaped, dumbfounded. Magnificent objects were crammed into every corner of the room. Exotic carvings jostled for space on ornate furniture. A fabulously coloured tapestry hung lopsidedly from the wall. And was that some kind of musical instrument strung from the hook in the corner?

No one had been inside the room for years. A film of dust lay over every surface. The room smelt musty. No breeze stirred the air, no sunlight lit the shadows that lurked in every corner.

The only sound in the ancient room was the slow, rhythmic tick of a large clock standing by the wall. How strange that it should still be going after all these years . . .

All of a sudden, the clock whirred and clanked into action. It began to strike the hour. One . . . Two . . . Three . . . Four . . . Five . . . Six . . . Seven . . . Eight . . . Nine . . . Ten . . . Eleven . . . Twelve . . .

The echo of the last stroke died away. Ant looked at his watch. "Twelve?" he said, puzzled. Then the door into the room slammed shut behind them.

The musical instrument in the corner swung slowly on its hook. One by one the rusted old strings began to tauten, then break. A strange-looking statue, perched on a table, jerked slowly into action. Round and round it danced as if by clockwork. Then the old scroll hanging from the wall started to flap and flutter on its hook.

"W-what's happening?" said Sally. A cold breath brushed the back of her neck. She cowered against the door, shivering with fright.

Sudden sunlight pierced the gloom. It was as if shafts of bright light were streaming in through a window – a window that was no longer there. Then a blast of icy air howled into the room and whistled past Ant and Sally.

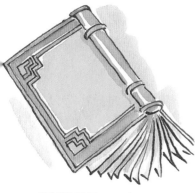

CLUNK! The wind snatched a book from the bookcase. The heavy tome fell to the floor with a thud. A shower of dust flew out of its crinkled pages.

The brilliant shaft of light blazed down on the old book. The wind whirled round and round it in angry gusts. Could the ancient pages hold some kind of clue to the mystery?

Sally bent to pick up the book. The wind died away and, for a moment, all was silent.

SSSSS! From the corner, there was a faint hissing, whining noise. It grew louder and louder. Ant and Sally span round. The noise was coming from an old-fashioned radio perched on a table in the corner.

The radio started to crackle into life. Quietly, so quietly that at first they couldn't make out the words, a faint, disembodied voice began to speak . . .

Stone . . . Hurry . . .
Read the diary . . .
But beware . . .
Enemy in house . . .
Hurry . . .

31

Max Takes Charge

Ant and Sally shot out of the room as fast as their wobbling legs would let them. Sally was still clutching the book she had picked up. "Look," she gasped. "It's a diary . . . Remember the radio message!" They stared at the battered old book. Could a vital clue to the missing Stone lurk in its dusty pages? Just then they heard footsteps approaching.

Beaming proudly, Max appeared round the corner. He was full of his plans for the day. Ant and Sally were aghast. But there was no escape.

Following Max's wobbly lead they headed down the winding lane on the ancient trikes he had dug out for them. At the village cafe, Max suggested they stop and have lunch. He was soon tucking in to a generous portion of gooseberry tartlet with spicy tomato relish.

Time ticked away. Ant's burger turned cold on its plate. Sally's sandwich curled up at the corners. Would Max never finish eating? They must find the Stone before the ancient curse claimed its next victim!

With a sigh of pleasure Max mopped the last traces of tomato off his chin. "Let's go!" he said. Ant and Sally jumped up. Free at last! But Max had plenty more entertainment in store back at Twelve Bells End.

Out in the garden Max began to explain the finer points of the first game. Ant racked his brains for a way to sound him out about the Stone. At last he blurted out a question, but Max ignored him. It was as if he hadn't heard a word Ant said.

Max seemed to find nothing strange about the games he had organized. Spin the Potty was followed by some slug racing. After a nail-biting finish Sally's slug, Desmond, was declared the winner. He was awarded a rosette.

Game followed game. Would they ever manage to get away? They played Hunt the Tarantula, Pass the Partridge, Hide and Squeak . . . Then, at last, dusk started to fall.

The first violent sheets of rain were lashing down on to the garden as they headed inside. Max had a musical evening planned. He performed movingly on the harp then led everyone in some spirited singing.

Sally looked anxiously at her watch. "We *must* read the diary," she hissed to Ant under cover of a noisy sea shanty. "Time is running out!"

33

The Diary

Half an hour later Ant and Sally managed to get away. They rushed back to their room. Sally picked up the diary. It fell open at the final entry and several bits of paper dropped out. They proved to be some very interesting bits of paper indeed . . .

FLOGGIT & QUICK

Valuation: Midnight Stone

Estimated resale value:

— Stone	£7,300
— Stone in setting	£10,560

Less our commission @ 40%   £4,380

Total:

— Stone	£6,336
— Stone in setting	

'Tis passing strange they have noe p nor X

Purchase — mandolin string, leeches, red hose

Top cop cops it!

Inspector Smug, the Yard's newest recruit, has been at the centre of a major scandal this week. This follows complaints of unlawful arrest by 42 members of the public in the last three months.

Smug admits to an arrest rate over 37% above the force average. The cuff-happy cop, whose previous jobs included a spell as quality controller for Tuffaware All-Weather Anoraks, transferred to the force seven years ago. A rapid rise

SMUG: too eager

through the ranks led to his promotion early last year.

A spokesman commented: "It happens sometimes. You get these newly promoted officers, keen as mustard – and a bit high-handed. The officer in question has been severely reprimanded."

This one looks promising!

Happy days for my Darling sons on the lake

The wind howled round the house and thunder grumbled angrily in the distance while they pored over the diary. Sloth prowled around the room, hissing uneasily, but they hardly noticed. Then something caught Sally's eye. "Look," she said excitedly, "Look at the date of the diary entry!"

12 November

Late start to the day after long night at the club with Stinker Harris. Such comfort in congenial company! He seems well content with his new post as Executioner General.

Spent much of day seeking a suitable place to keep 'CZN' safe from prying eyes. I fancy I have been successful, for who would seek to find what is no longer there?

First word from my small son! I held a shiny new sovereign in my hand. His tiny face looked up at me and 'Mine!' his little voice piped sweetly. I swear I felt a tear come pricking to my eye.

One amusing incident. Stumbled upon Forthright tending to the Rose Walk. Plucking a thorn, I thrust it into his flank - how high he jumped! And with what mirth my dearest wife, Magnolia, and I did laugh!

But alas, too little merriment these days, since M was banished in disgrace. With what strange sentiments I am afflicted. Sometimes I see his face before me. I wish to cry 'Forgive me!', but the words die on my lips. I walk beside the lake - it was there I thought up the idea - but it is a sad and melancholy place since his departure.

Now cast aside these thoughts! I feel, dear diary, weary and must lay down my pen. There is a sense of brooding in the air tonight. Sleep, I fancy, will be hard to come by.

Memorandum

To:
All staff
From:
Melrose Midnight

It has come to my attention that staff are exceeding their more than generous victual allowance. This must not continue. Staff issue is as follows:

Breakfast (5.30 am)
Porridge: 2 teaspoons
Salt: 7 grains (sugar on Sundays)
Luncheon (12.00 pm)
Boiled bacon rinds: ½ oz
Cabbage stalks: 3 (4 on Sundays)
Dinner (4.45 pm)
Bread and dripping: 1 slice
Apple: 2½ oz (including core)

In addition, smiling while going about duties is to be discouraged as unnecessary and unappealing.

Commander and Mrs Jacks
invite
Melrose Midnight
to celebrate
the marriage of their daughter
Polly
to
The Rt Hon Hugo Dellowes

SPRATTS
Quality outfitters
since 1793

To sale of: one pair
white gloves, finest kid
Remittance: 12/6

Yr earliest attention
respectfully requested

With thanks

Jack Spratt

The Pointing Finger

A nt looked at the date on the final diary entry. Something about the date jogged his memory. Of course! Suddenly it all fell into place . . . The twelfth of November: the night of the fire, the night the twelfth Lord Midnight put the curse on the house . . . The twelfth of November: the night of cousin Mervin's accident, and of Aunt Posy's – and of all the other accidents to members of the Midnight family . . . They all happened on the twelfth of November, and all at midnight!

"But," faltered Ant, "That's today's date. We've only got two hours left to find the Stone and break the curse before it happens again!"

Little did Ant and Sally know that the sinister housekeeper was skulking outside the door. With her ear glued to the keyhole, she could hear every word they said . . .

Then, from down the corridor, there was a faint whirring noise. The clock in the secret room once more started to strike.

Inside their room Ant and Sally hardly noticed the distant noise. Desperately they scoured the final diary entry for clues.

Ant had a thought. The Stone was made from cyanozine. Could "CZN" be a secret code for the Stone? But then what was the meaning of ". . . for who seeks to find what is no longer there"?

DONG! The hidden clock struck twelve. Sally felt an idea starting to form.

The secret room . . . The room that "is no longer there"!

They must have missed something. The clue to the Stone *had* to be in the secret room. They must go back!

If Ant and Sally had listened, they would have heard the sound of pounding feet running away. But they had forgotten about the crackling message on the radio, about the voice that warned them of an enemy in the house.

Outside the house, the rain battered against the ancient brickwork. A loud clap of thunder shook the old stone walls. Inside the hidden room, the temperature was icy. But was it only the cold that made them shiver as they looked around the dark and gloomy room?

All of a sudden, two ancient candles encrusted with age-old drips of wax, burst into flame. Sinister shadows and shapes filled the room, darting and flickering into every corner. Sally quivered with fear. Had a strange shadowy figure just flitted past her? And was that a faint voice whispering her name? "Sally, Sally. Turn round . . . Face the portrait. Look at the portrait."

With a terrified shudder, Sally turned to face the portrait. Staring down from the grimy frame were two figures: twin brothers . . .

Sally gasped. Was it a trick of the light or had the figures just moved? Then the figures moved again. Now one of the twins was pointing urgently at a statue. Meanwhile, the other twin scowled down with an expression of great menace.

Sally had seen the statue in the portrait before, in the garden. Could this be the end of the trail at last? Did the answer to the disappearance of the ancient gem lie outside in the wild and stormy night?

A Cryptic Clue

The wind howled and shrieked through the trees as Ant and Sally raced down the garden. Driving rain lashed at their faces. Above them, swollen thunderclouds scudded angrily through the stormy skies.

A flash of lightning seared across the dark and sinister garden. Ahead, glimmering eerily in the stormy light, they could see the ancient statue. Would this be the end of their search? They ran towards it. Then a giant burst of thunder crashed and rolled round the garden.

The cold, unblinking eyes of the old stone statue stared straight ahead as, with freezing fingers, they prodded and poked in every nook and cranny. Water trickled down their necks and seeped up through their shoes. They grew icy cold. It was hopeless. There was no sign of the ancient stone.

"Let's go back," shouted Sally above the noise of the wailing wind and swaying trees. "There's nothing here!" But speeding back to the house through the menacing shadows, neither of them noticed what a strange time of night it was for a woodcutter to be at work . . .

Back inside the secret room, dripping and chilled to the bone, they racked their brains desperately. Had they, somewhere, missed a clue? Ant stared at the portrait. A glimmer of an idea was forming in his head. "Maybe," he said slowly, "The figure isn't pointing at the statue at all . . ."

Maybe the figure is pointing at the frame itself!

There's something stuck in the back!

The moment Ant spoke, the picture started to shake and rattle on its hook. It shuddered from side to side, as if it was locked in some violent battle. Sally stretched up and grabbed the edges of the frame, then heaved as hard as she could. Tottering, she lowered the picture off the wall. With trembling fingers, she levered the back away from the frame. And there, wedged inside was a dusty piece of paper, tightly folded.

Ant lifted the paper out and unfolded it. The crinkled old sheet felt as if it might crumble to bits in his hands. Gingerly, he smoothed it out and stared down at the torn sheet. The spindly handwriting was all too familiar to both of them . . . They began to read. Would this, at last, lead them to the hiding place of the Midnight Stone?

Of many sides but single voice,
In rhythm but no rhyme,
Once hear me sing and you will find
I hold the key to time.

Bewildered, they reached the end of the mysterious message. It was some kind of poem, but it seemed to make no sense. What could it mean?

Outside, the wind still raged round the old house. It tore some old slate tiles from the roof and flung them to the ground, shattering them into tiny pieces. And all the while, time was edging closer and closer to midnight .

The End of the Search

A deafening roll of thunder shook the old house to its foundations. Ant and Sally huddled, shivering, inside the secret room. Again and again they read through the puzzling lines of the strange poem.

What was it they should look for? Something that could sing? Could that mean a musical instrument? But something with many sides? Was there anything inside this room that fitted that description? . . . At the same moment they both sprang into action.

There was no time to lose. Frantically, they searched the room. It *had* to be in here. But they found nothing. Then, almost despairing, Sally picked up a six-sided brown box and opened the lid .

At once, the eerie strains of a scraping stringed instrument filled the room. It was unlike anything Ant or Sally had heard before. Inside the box, sad-faced figures looped and twirled to the mournful tune.

Ant and Sally stood spellbound. Then a faint voice whispered, "It's a trick! Don't listen to the music."

Ant blinked. Something glinted inside the box. And there, cleverly hidden, was "the key to time"!

Now, should you seek a hiding place
These lines shall hold the answer.
Look for the courtier who ne'er
A step doth take, though dancer.

There, cloak'd in velvet secrecy,
Lies cloister'd from all sight
A precious stone, whose colour hides
Deeds darker than the night.

Ant grabbed the key. But what did it open? . . . Of course! He ran over to the clock. Fumbling, he pushed the key into the lock and turned it. The door swung open. Inside, the pendulum ticked slowly from side to side. Tucked away, they could see the edge of another torn sheet of paper.

Sally pulled it out. It was the rest of the riddle! They puzzled over the cryptic lines. Then they heard a faint voice urge, "Over here! Over here!"

BANG! The clock door slammed shut. The lights began to flicker. Then a sharp hissing noise, like an angry intake of breath, echoed round the room. But above the noise they heard the faint voice still calling to them. Ant and Sally span round towards the voice. Immediately Ant spotted something. "Look. The courtier!" he gasped.

Ant picked up the statue from the chest. He turned it over and over in his hands. But where was the Stone? There seemed to be no possible hiding place.

WOOOSH! A violent gust of icy wind swept the statue out of his hands. It crashed on to the floor and split in two – and there was something hidden inside . . .

Peeking out from between the two shattered halves was the corner of a dark blue velvet bag. Sally grabbed it. Trembling, she untied the knot.

Her fingers scrabbled inside the opened bag. She touched something – something cold as marble, smooth as silk. With trembling hands, she pulled it out of the bag . . .

Chaos Reigns

They had found the Midnight Stone at last! They stood marvelling at its dazzling beauty. Shimmering lights in shades of blue glowed off its smooth surface. But could they return the Stone to its rightful resting place before the final stroke of midnight? There were just five minutes left.

"Follow me," said Sally. Clutching the precious stone, she raced down into the hallway. There, perched high above them on the wall, was the relic.

It was hopeless. Sally's fingers groped helplessly just a few inches out of reach of the relic. But help was at hand. At that moment the professor came down the stairs. Anxiously, Sally held out the Stone. Smiling, he took it. Then chaos broke out.

KERRANG! A mirror flew off the wall and shattered on the floor. Sloth began to yowl. A great wind whistled into the hallway. It circled and whirled around the professor in violent gusts, spinning him round and round like a helpless toy top.

The noise was deafening. And, above it all, Sally thought she could hear a faint ghostly cry. But was it a cry of triumph or of anger?

The great wind howled round the hallway like some maddened wild beast. Outside a fork of lightning streaked past the window. They heard a mighty cracking noise. An ancient oak, standing sentinel for centuries past, had crashed to the ground.

DONG! Far away in the secret room, the clock started to chime. And on the twelfth stroke, the ancient curse would claim another victim . . .

Suddenly, a dark shadow loomed towards Ant, Sally and the professor. They cowered away, horror-struck. A sinister figure they recognized only too well moved nearer and nearer, arms outstretched to grab at the Stone . . .

A Sorry Tale

With one swift movement the housekeeper snatched the Stone from the professor – and replaced it in the relic. Just then the clock tolled the final stroke of midnight.

"No-o-o!" A ghostly howl of despair filled the hallway. Everyone stood immobile, chilled to the bone by the unearthly scream that ricocheted from wall to wall. Then the final anguished echoes faded away and all was silent.

Ant and Sally shivered. A faint, whispering voice, a whispering voice they had both heard before, began to echo through the hallway. "At last, at last, at last!", the faint voice whispered triumphantly, before it too died away.

For a moment everyone was dumbstruck, too dazed to move or speak . . . or almost everyone.

44

What Happened Next . . .

The housekeeper smiled. "My name is Marcia Midnight," she began. "My father was Maurice, disinherited twin brother of the twelfth Lord Midnight."

"When my father was banished, accused of stealing the Stone, he went to Mythika," she continued. "He got a job there as a lifeguard. That's how he met my mother. He saved her when a sea urchin punctured her water wings. They married within a fortnight. A year later, I was born. I was their only child."

Marcia Midnight rummaged in her apron and proudly produced a framed snapshot.

"My father never talked of the past," she went on. "Until, just before he died, he told me of his suspicions of his brother's treachery. I vowed to find proof to clear my father's name. I saw the job as housekeeper advertised. It seemed the perfect cover for some sleuthing. That was five months ago."

Tell me, Mrs Mopps, have you had much experience of French polishing?

"I soon realized that some strange spell hung over the people in the house. Then I stumbled on some papers that showed someone was stealing from each and every inmate. But who? The crook had covered his tracks well."

Marcia Midnight sat back exhausted, then continued. "Was there, I wondered, some connection between the strange spell and the fraud?"

"When you two arrived I put you in the room that the twelfth Lord Midnight and my father shared when they were boys. And that's when things started happening. From then on I followed your every move. The diary you found cleared my father's name. But there was no time to reveal the truth. The Stone had to be found! Then the professor made his fatal mistake . . ."

A cape!

The caped stranger!

Marcia Midnight dabbed at her eyes with a fine linen handkerchief, then spoke again. "Now my father is at peace, thanks to you. I know he would want you to have this."

She handed Ant and Sally a bulky bundle. "It was his favourite garment," she said, with a small and mysterious smile . . .

The next day Ant and Sally woke late. They dressed quickly and went downstairs. Max was alone in the dining room, sitting at the huge oval table. "Morning," he said. "Come and have some breakfast."

Ant and Sally sat down. They gaped around them at the transformation. Gone were the peculiar meals of the last few days. On the table were fruit juices, toast, cereal . . . And Max sat chewing on a croissant as if the strange and sinister events of the last few days had never taken place.

"All back to normal then?" asked Ant. But Max just looked at him blankly.

And whoever they spoke to, it was the same story. No one seemed to know what they were talking about. Posy Tutu was back at the barre, cousin Mervin was balancing his books . . . Everyone was behaving just as if nothing had happened. They didn't appear to remember anything at all.

Ant and Sally stared at each other, confused. Had it all been a dream?

Then Marcia Midnight appeared. "Follow me," she said, beckoning.

She led them to the secret room. But now the door was scrubbed. A shiny key twinkled in the lock. Inside, the window had been replaced. Beams of sunlight streamed on to furniture gleaming with polish. The place was spotless.

"There's something I thought you'd like to see," said Marcia Midnight. And then once more she smiled . . .

47

Did You Spot?

You can use this page to help you spot things that could be useful in solving the mystery. First, there are hints and clues you can read as you go along. They will give you some idea of what to look out for. Then there are extra notes you can read to check if you missed any of the details.

Hints and Clues

3   The letter might not make much sense now but, who knows, it could be useful later.

6-7   A caped stranger? Will he reappear?

8-9   Some things in the hallway could be worth remembering. Listen out for that clock. It could strike again . . . but what hour?

10-11   Are you seeing double in the bedroom? Surely it's not long since the clock last struck? Have you noticed how loud it is?

12-13   Are they all bonkers? That's a lot of money one of them has tucked in a pocket.

14-15   Is it really midnight? Have you looked at the book and the mirror?

16-17   These dates and times might be useful. Keep your eyes open for familiar faces.

18-19   Is there another early riser in the house? The villagers seem concerned about time.

20-21   What could Lord Midnight want to save so much? Did you read his last words carefully? Did you notice the time?

22-23   Have you recognized anything in the book? Cyanozine: a name to remember . . .

24-25   So it was Lord Midnight who rang Smug. Is there an eavesdropper about? Frank has doubts about the evidence. Take a good look at the family group watching Smug leave.

26-27   A secret room - but where? Could Ant be right to feel niggled? How well the caped stranger seems to know the lake.

28-29   Did you spot the newer brickwork? Have you looked at the window next to it? Did you notice the falling gargoyle?

30-31   The portrait could be worth studying. The radio message has some good advice.

32-33   Spin the Potty has quite an audience.

34-35   There seems plenty of useful and useless information here. Can you sort it out? Watch out for clues to the Stone.

36-37   Is the housekeeper alone in the corridor?

38-39   A mystery woodcutter and a branch that just misses them . . . remember the radio warning. Do you recognize the writing?

40-41   A musician may help you find the key.

42-43   How strange, the professor suddenly seems to have no need for his ear trumpet.

By the Way . . .

Did you notice:

. . . the clock strike midnight and the air turn icy cold before ghostly activity?

. . . the ghostly powers of Maurice Midnight getting stronger as the hour of the curse drew nearer?

. . . the evil ghost of the twelfth Lord Midnight appear as Ant and Sally got close to the Stone?

. . . quantum physicist Guy ffoulkes (Sunday Scorcher) has opened a fish shop in Middle-Knight-on-Sea? Whose ghost did he see, do you think?

. . . Hollywood actress Faye Slift and her faithful pooch Clapperboard (Sunday Scorcher) in the train, on the village green and at the cafe?

. . . news of Tuffaware All-Weather Anoraks (Smug's ex-employer, page 34) in the Sunday Scorcher?

. . . the invitation to Polly Tack's wedding (page 35)? She becomes Councillor Polly Bellowes (Sunday Scorcher).

More about the Midnight Family

Did you work out who everyone was? (If not, reread pages 10, 12 and 16.) Sitting clockwise round the table from Sally on page 12, they are: Posy Tutu, Juster Chuckle, Mervin Midnight, Myrtle and Harvey, Merle, the professor.

You might like to know how Myrtle and Harvey fell foul of the ancient curse. Many years ago as they danced a military waltz at their wedding party, a chandelier crashed down from the ceiling and landed on the nuptial pair as the clock struck midnight. Merle was a more recent victim. Two years ago, she tripped at midnight on the trailing strands of a large cobweb and tumbled downstairs.

In case you wondered about the portraits on page 10: Modesty is married to Juste (she was away on a costume design course from 11-13 November); the man in hiking gear is Milo, who patented the first typewriter to use Mythikan script; John is chief photographer at the Mythikan court and current darling of the society ladies.

Incidentally, the family villa is in Tiktoki, a small village on the Mythikan coast. And did you spot the Mythikan influence in the secret room?

GHOST TRAIN
TO NOWHERE

Phil Roxbee Cox

Illustrated by
Jane Gedye

Contents

The Arrival

When twins Alf and Chrissy first saw their Uncle Jack's house, they were in for a surprise. "You live in a station!" gasped Chrissy.

"It used to be a station," nodded Uncle Jack, lifting their luggage out of his car. "But a train hasn't stopped in Seabry for over eighty years." The twins picked up their backpacks and followed their uncle onto the old station platform. Chrissy was sure she heard the distant hoot of an owl.

That's odd, she thought. Owls are night birds. Even though it was a blazing hot summer's day, a cold shiver ran down her spine. Suddenly, the leaves on the trees in the nearby wood began to rustle, but there was no wind. In fact, there was an odd stillness in the air.

Both twins were overcome by a strange feeling. It was a feeling of excitement and anxiety and of mysterious things to come . . .

The Broken Pane

Passing through the front door, the twins immediately sensed that they were being watched. A pair of unblinking eyes stared at them through a small window in the wall to their right.

"Meet Salmon," said Uncle Jack. "He's one in a long line of cats who has lived in this station. Station cats used to be paid an official wage to catch rats and mice."

They were standing in a large room crammed full of furniture. The twins looked around in interest.

"This used to be the waiting room," Uncle Jack explained.

"So that must have been the old ticket office," said Alf, walking over to where Salmon was sitting, watching them closely. The twins explored their new surroundings. Every picture, every ornament and every book had something to do with trains.

"Where are we going to sleep?" Alf asked. Uncle Jack pointed to a door marked 'LEFT LUGGAGE OFFICE'. Chrissy could feel Salmon's big green eyes following her as she walked over to it. She shivered again. Why did such a bright and cheerful house make her feel so strangely cold? It didn't make sense.

In their bedroom they found shelves of dusty trunks and suitcases left by passengers long ago, never to be reclaimed. Uncle Jack left the twins to unpack their own things, and went to boil some eggs.

Alf stuffed all his clothes into one drawer, then went over to the window. He looked out at the wooded valley sloping into the distance and wondered where the trains used to go once they left the station.

"The old track might still be out there," he said, then leaped back in surprise.

Without the slightest sound, a crack was slowly forming in the glass. It was zig-zagging its way up the middle of the window, only inches from Alf's face.

Chrissy looked on in utter amazement.

Something in the Woods

Uncle Jack claimed he wasn't bothered by the broken window. "It was probably the heat," he said. "The sun has been shining on it all day. Sometimes, if it gets too hot, glass cracks like that . . . especially glass around here." Alf and Chrissy were unconvinced by his explanation. He was studying them with a strange look in his eyes. Then again, it could just have been a trick of the light.

That night, Alf lay in bed staring up at the ceiling. Silvery moonlight shone through the window and the flimsy curtain, projecting the crack onto the ceiling as a jagged black line. He couldn't take his eyes off it.

Then something made him climb out of bed and pull back the curtain. It wasn't a voice in his head, but a sudden *need* to look out into the night. Chrissy opened a bleary eye. "Close the curtain will you? Some of us are trying to sleep," she groaned, lifting the bedclothes over her head.

As Alf was pulling the curtain back across the window, he caught sight of a puff of smoke coming from the woods.

"Chrissy!" he said in a harsh whisper. "Wake up."

"I wasn't asleep," said his sister. She joined him at the window and saw the smoke. "What's the big deal?" she asked. "Perhaps someone is camping out there in the woods and . . ." She stopped and pulled the curtain urgently across the window.

"What's the matter with you?" Alf asked.

"I've felt weird since we arrived, and now I've got the feeling that we're being watched," said Chrissy. "And what about that owl hoot in broad daylight?" She made a hooting noise by blowing air through her cupped hands.

TOOT!

"There *is* something freaky about this place," Alf admitted. He looked at the shadowy shapes of the long-forgotten luggage on the shelves. "Maybe it's having all this old stuff around us. It's exciting but creepy at the same time."

Alf couldn't get the image of the crack out of his mind. Glass didn't crack like that, so slowly and so silently. He felt the hairs on the back of his neck begin to rise . . . Now he too had a strong sense of being watched. He peered around the edge of the curtain into the silvery moonlight. Above the trees, the smoke had drifted away to nothing in the night air.

"I think we should investigate the smoke in the morning," said Chrissy. Something buried deep in her mind told her that the reason for their uneasiness lay out there in the woods. They would have to find out what it was if they didn't want any more sleepless nights.

Meanwhile, unknown to the twins, a shadowy figure lurked at the edge of the woods, avoiding the light of the moon. He stood in silence, watching and waiting, but waiting for what? And why?

The Stranger

The next morning, the twins had breakfast with Uncle Jack in the tiny kitchen that used to be the ticket office. Then they set off to explore the woods.

I've boiled you some eggs.

They walked through the trees until they reached a clearing at the bottom of a steep bank. "It's an old path," said Chrissy.

"Not a path," said Alf excitedly. "This must be where the old track used to be. Steam trains used to run along here."

"I wonder why they closed down the track?" Chrissy thought out loud.

"That's a very good question," said a voice. It was a dry, rasping voice. The voice of a stranger. The twins spun around. The voice belonged to an old man clutching a walking stick.

"You shouldn't have sneaked up on us like that," gulped Chrissy.

The stranger smiled. "I'm sorry," he said. "I took the easy route. You could have followed this old track straight from your uncle's house."

Chrissy felt that there was something odd about the old man. "How do you know who we are?" she asked suspiciously. "You just said our *uncle's* house."

I didn't mean to alarm you.

The stranger smiled. "There's no mystery in that," he said. "Seabry is a small village where everybody knows everybody else. My name is Harold Masters. I'm a very good friend of your uncle's. He told me that his twin nephew and niece were coming to stay. In fact, I've been looking forward to meeting you very much."

Chrissy felt stupid for not having trusted Harold Masters. Of course Uncle Jack would have told his friends that they were coming. She asked the old man if he had seen any smoke in the woods. The change that came over him was incredible. His eyes lit up with excitement and he pressed his face right up against hers. "You've seen smoke?" he asked urgently, as if it was the most important question in the world.

"Yes. Last night," said Alf. "From our bedroom window."

At that moment, there was an enormous clap of thunder, like some massive explosion, and a bolt of forked lightning seemed to split the clear blue sky in two. The blinding flash of light struck the branch of a tall tree to their left, setting it alight and ripping it from the trunk.

The blackened burning branch hurtled down toward them, flames streaking out like a comet's tail. "Look out!" screamed Alf.

The Thurhorn Bridge Disaster

It was a lucky escape. The huge branch only narrowly missed them. Chrissy felt the heat of the flames as it passed her face. There was a stunned silence, then Alf quickly helped Harold Masters to his feet. The old man had tripped in the scramble to save himself. Chrissy handed him his walking stick. The twins were shaking.

Thank you. I'm fine. I'm tougher than I look.

"If that had hit us . . ." began Alf.

"There's no point dwelling upon it," said Mister Masters. He seemed less surprised than the twins that a bolt of lightning should suddenly flash out of a clear blue sky. He ignored the blackened branch that still smouldered at their feet.

Chrissy turned and looked around her. There was an absolute stillness in the woods and no birds sang. "There's something strange about this place," she said. "It's quiet . . . too quiet . . . Something's *wrong*."

The twins could feel the old man's piercing eyes studying them intently. He cleared his throat. "Perhaps you could help put things right," he rasped.

"What do you mean?" asked Alf. The forked lightning had reminded him of the shape of the crack that had appeared in the window.

Harold Masters paused for a while before answering. It was as though he was trying to decide whether to share a secret with them or not. "I only know so much, and no more," he sighed. Chrissy noticed the old man had tears in his eyes.

"Does it have anything to do with the old track?" she asked. She didn't know what had made her ask that, or where the question even came from. The words just tumbled out of her mouth without her thinking.

Harold Masters nodded. "It has *everything* to do with the old track," he said, and told them a tragic tale . . .

When I was a boy, there were trains running up and down this track all the time. It was a very busy line.

All aboard!

Everyone in the village was proud of its station and the line that ran to Thurhorn.

Running like clockwork as usual.

Then, one winter's evening, disaster struck. My twin brother caught the 7:15 train from Seabry to Thurhorn. A terrible storm had been raging all day.

'Bye Harry.

'Bye Bill.

What nobody knew was that part of the bridge between here and Thurhorn had been washed away when the river burst its banks.

The train never reached Thurhorn. Nobody knows exactly what happened next, but an official inquiry said that it must have driven full speed off the end of the bridge. I never saw my brother again.

A Discovery

Neither Chrissy nor Alf knew what to say when the old man had finished his sorry story. He stood up and stared into the distance. "The bridge is some miles in that direction." He pointed. "This wood is so overgrown in parts that you'd get lost trying to follow the old track."

"Were there any survivors?" asked Alf, imagining the train plummeting to its watery grave.

"We never even found the train," said Harold Masters. "When it didn't arrive in Thurhorn, a search party from Seabry went out in the storm and found part of the bridge destroyed."

"The next day, the search party dragged the river and I was there, watching from the bank. They found nothing. The train and everyone on it was thought to have been washed out to sea by the raging torrent of the swollen river. The company closed the line soon after that. Since then, no earthly train has passed this way."

No sign of them.

They didn't stand a chance.

"*Earthly* train?" said Alf, mystified. "What do you mean? It's very sad Mister Masters, but what does it have to do with what's happening now? "

The old man frowned and studied the twins' faces before he spoke. "Perhaps things are about to change. Perhaps you can help. Nobody has ever believed me you see, but maybe you will . . . and things may start happening around here." With that, he walked away. "Come to my house tomorrow," he called over his shoulder. "Your uncle knows where I live."

Before Harold Masters was even out of sight, Alf turned to Chrissy and said: "We must follow the old track. Don't ask me why, I just *feel* we must." Chrissy didn't argue. She felt it too.

Let's go this way. It looks like the track passed between those trees.

Good idea.

The farther they went, the more overgrown and difficult it was for the twins to follow the route of the old track. By late afternoon, there was no sign of where the track used to run, so they could only guess which way to go. By early evening, they were well and truly lost.

"We should have turned back when we still had a track to follow," sighed Chrissy. Her feet were aching from all the walking. She began to suspect that they'd been going around in circles. Then it started to rain.

"Brilliant," said Alf. "That's all we need."

Chrissy spotted what looked like a large cave in the hillside up ahead. "We can shelter in there," she said. As they got nearer, the twins realized that the cave wasn't a cave at all. It had brickwork around the edges. Alf broke into a run, dashing past his sister in the pouring rain.

We can take shelter in there.

He couldn't contain his excitement. "It's not a cave." he cried, fighting his way through a rain soaked bush. "We're back on course. It's the entrance to an old tunnel!"

Into the Hillside

"This is amazing," said Alf, his voice echoing into the eerie blackness beyond. "Even the track itself is still here. Look!" He pointed at the huge wooden sleepers. The twins stepped into the tunnel.

The more they walked, the darker and more uninviting their surroundings became. A strange smell hung in the air and strands of sooty black cobwebs brushed against their faces as they ventured into the unknown.

"Let's come back tomorrow when it's brighter," suggested Chrissy.

"We may never find our way back here," said Alf. He wanted to go on exploring. He felt as though the track itself was drawing him in deeper and deeper. There was no turning back now.

Chrissy walked back to the mouth of the tunnel to see if it was still raining. She sat on one of the sleepers and watched the water pouring through the trees. Alf plunged even farther into the hillside, thinking about the storm that had destroyed part of Thurhorn Bridge all those years before.

Alf found alcoves at regular intervals along the walls. He guessed that these must have been spaces that workmen stood in when they heard a train coming. Alf stepped into one of the alcoves and imagined what it must have been like with a steam locomotive thundering by.

His eyes were attracted by a glint of metal on the ground. Brushing cobwebs from his face, he bent down to investigate. It was a silver whistle on a long chain.

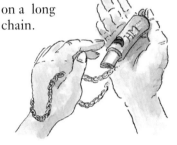

Alf ran back to the tunnel entrance so that he could show Chrissy what he'd found. "I think it's made of silver," he said. "I expect it's quite old. It must have been used by a guard when trains still ran through here."

Chrissy studied the whistle and chain carefully. "It can't have been lying in here for very long," she said. "Look how bright and shiny it is. Silver turns all black after a time if you don't keep polishing it . . ."

A sudden hissing made Chrissy bite her tongue. Alf jumped with fright at the noise. Dreading what they might see, they slowly turned to look back into the yawning depths of the tunnel.

At first, they saw nothing. Then, out of nowhere, something was hurtling toward them at great speed. Two glowing yellow circles hung in the darkness, growing bigger and bigger as they got rapidly nearer. They couldn't be . . . it wasn't possible . . . Were these the lights of an oncoming train? The twins ran in blind panic.

The Chase

Chrissy and Alf spilled out into the daylight and the lashing rain, convinced that they were about to be confronted by some unearthly train.

Out in the open, they stopped to catch their breath. All the twins could hear was the sound of their own blood pumping through their veins. No hissing of steam. No ghostly wails. Cautiously, they made their way back to the tunnel entrance.

Their relief soon turned to a different kind of horror as a beast launched itself out of the darkness. It was just recognizable as a cat, but it wasn't like any other cat, or any other animal, either of them had ever seen. It was huge, with bald patches in its fur and it only had one ear. But what was really strange about this beast was its eyes. Glowing brighter than hot coals in a fire, they had no pupils. It snarled at the twins, curling back its gums to reveal a set of yellowing fangs, as it hurtled through the air toward Alf.

"Look out!" cried Chrissy, and her brother threw up his arms to defend himself against the creature's razorsharp claws. But the cat did not land on him. In one surprisingly graceful movement, it snatched the silver whistle and chain from his grasp, landed on the grass and dashed away. Alf was dumbfounded.

"Are you all right?" asked Chrissy. Alf nodded. The smell of the beast's breath still filled his nostrils. Beads of sweat had formed on his forehead.

The creature appeared in the nearby undergrowth, the whistle and chain hanging tantalizingly between its jaws. "We must get the whistle back," Alf shouted. "It could be important." Without even stopping to consider what they would do if they managed to catch the beast, the twins set off in hot pursuit.

They chased the cat for what seemed like miles. Sometimes they would lose sight of it and then its head would suddenly appear from behind a tree or pop up by a rock right next to them. It was almost as if the cat was playing with them, speeding ahead to make them follow then slowing down to let them keep up.

"I give up," said Alf at last, clutching his side and trying to catch his breath. He collapsed on a patch of wet grass. Looking across at Chrissy, he realized that it had stopped raining. Then he realized something far more important. "I know where we are!" he cried. "This is where we met Mister Masters. Look. There's the burned branch."

"You're right," laughed Chrissy. "The cat thought it was leading us around in circles, but it's almost led us home. The station isn't far from here."

When they reached the old station and climbed the steps to the platform, they were in for yet another surprise. Just outside the front doors lay the whistle and chain.

Chrissy looked down at the whistle and chain. Both were battered and the silver was tarnished with dull grey patches. "It's the same whistle for sure. It has the letters engraved on it, but it looks so much older. This is crazy!"

A Link with the Past

Uncle Jack was very excited when they showed him the whistle. He claimed that he was only interested in it as a piece of local history, but both Alf and Chrissy could tell that it meant more to him than that. There was a strange look in his eyes, and he wanted to know exactly where they had found it. He made the twins feel uneasy.

He went over to a shelf and pulled out an old photo album. He blew dust off it and flipped through the pages. "There," he said pointing to a black and white photograph of a man in a guard's uniform. He had a small flag in one hand and a whistle on a chain in the other. "In those days, all the guards would have had whistles like the one you found." Alf and Chrissy studied the old picture with interest. Their whistle certainly looked similar to the one in the guard's hand.

Uncle Jack handed Chrissy the whistle and she hung it around her neck on the chain. "You should show it to Mister Masters when you see him tomorrow morning," he said, and put the album back on the shelf. "You didn't find anything else did you?" he asked. "Or see anything? Nothing odd? No strange noises?" The twins felt awkward at this sudden stream of questions. They said nothing.

Uncle Jack frowned. "Is there something you're not telling me?" he demanded. There was a sense of urgency in his voice.

The twins looked at each other. They weren't going to tell him about the enormous cat with the glowing eyes . . . "Of course not," said Chrissy.

"Nothing out of the ordinary," Alf added. "Can we eat soon? I'm starving."

After a supper of three boiled eggs each, the twins went straight to their bedroom. Once they were inside the old Left Luggage Office, however, they didn't go to bed. They discussed the day's events in low whispers.

"I keep feeling the need to do things without quite knowing why," whispered Alf. "When we were in the tunnel I felt like a piece of metal being drawn to a huge magnet. Do you know what I mean?"

His sister nodded. "It's all somehow connected to the old Seabry-to-Thurhorn line. I know it is," said Chrissy. "And I bet Uncle Jack knows much more than he's letting on."

Chrissy was right. Little did they know that their uncle was lurking outside the door to the Left Luggage Office at that very moment. He stood very still, trying not to make a sound, straining to hear what they had to say about the day's events.

I must keep an even closer eye on those two from now on, he thought. I must be careful, very careful, or things could get out of hand.

Things of Interest

The next morning, Alf and Chrissy went to the home of Harold Masters. It was a tumbled down cottage at the edge of the village. Chrissy found a note pinned to the front door of the cottage. It read: TWINS. HAVE HAD TO GO OUT ON URGENT BUSINESS. PLEASE GO INSIDE. YOU WILL FIND SOME THINGS OF INTEREST ON THE TABLE. It was signed 'Harold Masters'.

Chrissy pushed open the door nervously. At first, they couldn't find the 'things of interest'. The only things on the table were old newspaper clippings. Then Chrissy noticed just how old the clippings were.

THURHORN BRIDGE DISASTER
Train crashes. No survivors.

In one of the worst storms this century, the river Thur burst its banks on Tuesday and washed away part of the Thurhorn Bridge viaduct. The bridge carries the line between the village of Seabry and Thurhorn. The 7:15pm train from Seabry, pulled by the steam locomotive *The Gypsy Bell*, is thought to have plummeted two hundred feet from the bridge into the river below. The Gravel Hill Rail Company say that there were thirty passengers and six crew members on board.

Sergeant Able Morris.

Sergeant Able Morris, who was in charge of the search party, told reporters: 'There is no sign of the train or its passengers or crew. The rain was so heavy and fell so quickly that the river Thur rose over ten feet in a matter of hours. I am sad to report that there is no hope of anyone having survived such a tragedy. I have never been interviewed by reporters before and would like to say hello to my mother and anyone else who reads what I have said.'

Thurhorn-to-Seabry line, famous for its many bends.

Masters Family sell Briary Manor

Jonathan Masters is to sell Briary Manor which has belonged to his family for over 200 years. Mr. Masters's lawyer, Mr. Ben Horace, said that it was with great regret that the manor was being put up for sale.

"Since the loss of his son William in the Thurhorn Bridge Disaster, Mr. Masters wishes to start a new life with his wife and remaining son, Harold, away from Seabry."

Identical twins Harold and William were a familiar sight to [lo]cal residents.

Briary Manor

"I have no doubt that the whole family will be sorely missed," said Mr. Horace.

"Look," she said. "These are over eighty years old. They're reports on the Seabry-to-Thurhorn line and the night of the storm."

"And if you're right about all the weird goings-on being connected to the old station and track . . ." began Alf.

"Exactly," his sister interrupted. "Then these old newspaper reports might give us some vital clues." They spread the clippings out on the table and read through them.

Famous Mystic Missing

The world famous mystic Marcus Hillcutty is thought to have been on the ill-fated train journey across the Thurhorn Bridge.

Marcus Hillcutty, who has performed mystical feats for presidents, royalty and anyone else with enough money to pay him, was going to Thurhorn for the annual meeting of The Society For Men With Impressive Beards of which he was President. He never arrived.

Marcus Hillcutty is probably most famous for making the fabulous Akimbo diamond disappear during a performance at the court of King Gulash of Gaberdeen. Unfortunately, he was unable to make it reappear, claiming that 'he was not as good at that part'. He narrowly avoided a prison sentence.

This year's meeting of The Society For Men With Impressive Beards has been cancelled out of respect for the missing mystic.

World famous Marc

SEABRY-TO-THURHORN LINE TO CLOSE

Following the recent Thurhorn Bridge disaster, the President of the Gravel Hill Rail Company has announced that the Seabry-to-Thurhorn line is to close.

'This is out of respect for those involved in the accident,' Sir Nigel Lyer said. 'It is not because we cannot afford to repair the bridge. Honestly.'

'GYPSY BELL' DRIVER WAS LOCAL MAN

The driver of the steam locomotive *The Gypsy Bell* which was pulling the 7:15 from Seabry was Samuel 'Safety' Stevens. He had lived in Seabry all his life and, until the accident, had the best safety record of all the drivers working for the Gravel Hill Rail Company.

'If anyone broke so much as a fingernail on one of his trains it was unusual,' said a company spokesman. 'If there was any way to save his passengers on that bridge, Mister 'Safety' Stevens would have done it. He was a professional and popular man.'

With him on the footplate was fireman Wally Walters whose job it was to stoke the boiler. The guard was Henry Moose another popular Seabry inhabitant. Moose's mother, Amanda Moose (64) is well known locally for her work with sick seagulls.

A sick seagull.

69

The Village of Lost Hope

The twins were puzzled by the newspaper clippings. They were about the Thurhorn Bridge disaster and nothing else. Surely Harold Masters had more to tell them than that? Alf and Chrissy felt none the wiser, and decided that the village itself might hold some clue.

Seabry turned out to be a sad place. A sense of gloom hung in the air. Time had been cruel to the village. What were once pretty houses and cottages were now neglected and decayed. Windows were broken, plaster was cracked and tiles were falling off roofs. In the middle of the village stood a monument with a statue of a steam locomotive on top. The twins went to take a closer look.

It's as if nobody cares about this place.

It's so dull and lifeless.

An inscription was carved into the old and crumbling stone, which read: IN MEMORY OF THE VICTIMS OF THE THURHORN BRIDGE DISASTER. When Alf walked around the monument, he discovered something else was written on the other side. He couldn't read it because it was covered with moss. "Did you bring your pocketknife?" he asked Chrissy.

Chrissy took a knife from her pocket and they began to scrape away the moss. Alf used his fingers. Soon they had uncovered the words: 'PLEASE HELP US'. The twins wondered what it could mean.

70

Alf looked at the gloomy, unloved houses surrounding the green. Fences were broken and rotting, and weeds grew through cracks in the paths. Even the ducks in the muddy village pond looked depressed. He decided that the place could certainly do with some help.

Chrissy interrupted his thoughts with a cry. "Look!" she said, pointing with a shaking hand at a second row of moss covered letters. They seemed to shimmer into place before their very eyes. "T-T-Those weren't there a moment ago!" Goose pimples rose on the twins' flesh and they felt icily cold.

Alf and Chrissy frantically set about scraping off the moss. Because the words were so familiar to them, they both knew what the letters spelled before they'd even cleaned them all. It was their own names.

Were they dreaming? Had they gone mad? The letters weren't freshly carved. They had been worn by the weather, and by time itself . . . but these were their names, and it was no coincidence. It was as if this was a desperate plea for help reaching out to them across the years.

Chrissy's head began to spin. She put her hand out to steady herself, and touched the statue of *The Gypsy Bell*. Her arm tingled violently, and everything around them became a whirling blur of sight and sounds.

Suddenly, Alf and Chrissy were plunged into total darkness and felt a gust of wind against their faces. There was the deafening screech of metal on metal. The air became thick with choking smoke, and light appeared out of nowhere. "Look out!" screamed Alf.

A Nightmare Journey

They were back in the tunnel! Alf grabbed Chrissy by the arm and pulled her into one of the alcoves, pressing himself flat against the cold slimy wall. A split second later, a steam train came screeching out of the empty darkness and thundered by, shaking the ground beneath them.

This was no ordinary train. It glowed like white-hot metal and was driven by a man with a crazed look in his eyes. Next to him on the footplate stood a second man, blackened with soot, frantically stoking the boiler with a shovel.

Grey and desperate faces seemed to stare from every window, eyes wide and helpless. A ghostlike child had his hands pressed against the glass.

As the locomotive reached the tunnel opening and daylight, it dissolved into nothing. Each of the four coaches in turn did the same. When the last coach disappeared, there was a deafening silence . . .

Tales to Tell

"**A**re you all right?" asked a familiar voice. Alf sat up, his head still spinning. He rubbed his eyes and looked into the concerned face of Harold Masters. They were on the village green.

"What have you two been up to?" asked the old man. "You're covered in soot." Alf and Chrissy looked at their clothes. He was right.

The twins were at a loss for words. They felt as though they had just woken from a deep sleep which they couldn't quite shake off. Standing up, the ground felt shaky underfoot and their minds felt scrambled.

Mister Masters insisted that they come back to his cottage. While Alf had a bath and Chrissy a shower, the old man proudly produced some clean clothes for them to wear. Later they all sat together in his huge red chairs.

Feeling clean but confused, Alf and Chrissy told the old man about the carved message asking them for help by name, and about the train. "It was a ghost train . . . It was there but, at the same time, it wasn't . . ." Chrissy finished.

"You probably think we're crazy," said Alf.

Harold Masters shook his head and smiled. "You couldn't be more wrong," he said. "What you've told me is exactly what I've been hoping to hear. For over eighty years most people in Seabry have thought *I* was crazy, but what you've just said changes everything. Let me explain . . ."

Alf and Chrissy had never really thought about there being a special bond between twins before. But what about those birthdays when they had bought each other exactly the same presents? Maybe that explained it. There could be some invisible force that linked one twin to another.

"But what we saw was a *ghost* train, Mister Masters," said Alf. "Doesn't that prove that your brother is . . . a ghost?"

"The writing on the monument was a plea for help," said Harold Masters with a faraway look. "And those able to ask for help are able to be saved!"

Revelations

I t was early evening when the twins left Harold Masters's cottage, their soot-covered clothes in a bag. They walked back toward the station, going over what the old man had told them.

"How can Mister Masters believe that his brother Bill is still out here somewhere?" asked Chrissy. "It doesn't make sense. Bill Masters was on that train when it crashed years ago, and now we've actually seen a train full of ghosts. What more proof does he want?"

Alf's eyes lit up. "That's it. Proof!" he cried. "What proof do we have that the train went over the end of Thurhorn Bridge in the storm? Think about it. According to Mister Masters and the newspaper clippings, nobody actually saw it go into the river and no wreck was ever found. Maybe it never happened!"

Chrissy frowned. "If it didn't go over the bridge, where did the train disappear to on the night of the storm? And if there wasn't an accident, why did we run into a train full of ghosts this afternoon?" Alf's idea seemed ridiculous but, at the same time, there was something about it that made a strange kind of sense.

"Oh well," sighed Alf. "It was just a thought." They arrived back at the station and went inside. Uncle Jack looked up from a large book he was reading.

"Hello," he smiled. "Perfect timing. Supper's ready."

How did you get in here?

The nightmare journey to the tunnel and back had left the twins exhausted. After supper, they were asleep within minutes of going to bed . . . then came the voices. Chrissy thought she was imagining things, until she saw Alf was also sitting up and listening. A chorus of desperate whispering filled the room. Words were spoken quickly and frantically until, quite suddenly, they fell silent and the twins remembered nothing else until morning.

They woke up bursting with energy. The sun was shining, Salmon was purring, and their heads were filled with new ideas and understanding. Now they somehow knew that they had been *chosen* to see and hear certain things. Had the whispering voices told them? Without speaking, both Alf and Chrissy hurried over to the window and looked out into the woods.

"The noise we've heard wasn't the hooting of an owl, but the tooting of the steam whistle on the ghost train," said Chrissy, looking past the crack in the glass to the trees beyond.

" I know,"Alf nodded. "But some things still need explaining. I mean, what does this cracked window have to do with a ghost train? Maybe it did just crack in the heat."

Chrissy stared at the crack and her eyes opened wide with excitement. "No, don't you see?" she cried. "Don't you see?"

Don't you see?

77

The Trek Through the Woods

Chrissy pointed at the crack. "It's a kind of map!" she said. "Perhaps there's a special place you need to stand for it to work. You try. Stand here." She stepped aside and Alf took her place. He was stunned. From the parts of the woods he could recognize, the crack lined up with the route of the old track. What mysterious force could create a crack in glass in such a precise pattern?

It's more of a picture than a map.

"I wonder if it's an instruction," Chrissy suggested. "It could be telling us to follow the old track. We turned back at the tunnel last time." Her heart was beating faster with excitement. Somehow she *knew* that she was right. Alf felt it too.

Just then, a large moth landed on the window, near the top of the crack in the glass. Chrissy tried to shoo it away with her hand. "No. Wait," said Alf. "If the crack is some kind of map, what does this moth look like?"

"Some weird kind of insect," said Chrissy, wondering what her brother was getting at.

"No. It looks like an X," said Alf. He could see a rock sticking up through the trees, past the moth. "We've got to go to this spot."

"We'll never find it," said Chrissy. "Don't forget how overgrown parts of the track are. And this isn't an ordinary map. We can't take it with us."

X marks the spot.

"We'll find a way, I'm sure of it," said Alf. "Let's go."

Uncle Jack was nowhere to be seen, so they grabbed what they needed without having to explain. They borrowed two old fashioned lanterns, in case they went back inside the tunnel, and hastily filled their backpacks, before dashing off into the woods. "Do you think we'll see the ghost train again?" asked Alf, with a slight tremor in his voice. Chrissy raised her eyebrows and shrugged her shoulders. Who knew what lay ahead of them . . . ?

They passed the blackened branch in the clearing where they'd first met Harold Masters, and walked deeper and deeper into the woods. Just when it became impossible to find the remains of the old track, there was a scrambling and rustling noise from the undergrowth. The beast with the glowing eyes came out from behind a bush and leaped onto a branch in front of them. It faced them with its blank expression but somehow seemed smaller, and far less threatening than before.

I think we're supposed to follow it.

Friend or foe?

The beast stood up and began to walk away, quickly followed by Alf and Chrissy who were afraid they might lose sight of it. They began to trust their guide, but this didn't stop them feeling nervous when they reached the yawning entrance to the tunnel. Gingerly, they stepped inside. No ghostly train appeared as they made their way through the blackness. They came out the other end unshaken, but blinking in the sunlight. Moments later, they were led to a clearing with a large outcrop of rock in the middle. They had reached the spot. What now?

H-Help!

Exhausted, Alf sat down and slipped off his backpack. "We're here," he said and turned just in time to see Chrissy being swallowed up by the ground. She let out a piercing scream.

Exploring Below

Chrissy blinked and tried to get used to the darkness. Where was she? What had happened? There was a small circle of light way above her, but that was all. She fumbled in her backpack and pulled out one of the lanterns and a box of matches. The match spluttered to life and the lantern flickered then gave off a red glow.

Holding the lantern high, Chrissy inspected her new surroundings. She had fallen into an underground cave of some sort, with the roof and walls supported by massive wooden props. Shadowy passages led off in all directions. The air smelled dank and musty. She shuddered.

"CHRISSEEEEE!" echoed a voice from above. Alf's face appeared through the hole in the roof. "Are you okay?" he called. His eyes hadn't had time to adjust to the dark, so all he could see was a red glow.

"Fine! A little bruised, that's all." Chrissy shouted. "Get the rope, and come on down."

Alf took the rope from his backpack and tied one end to a tree. He lowered the other end down the hole and climbed slowly into the gloom.

When he reached the bottom, Chrissy gave him the matches. Soon his lantern was giving off a green glow. He looked around in wide eyed amazement. "These tunnels could stretch for miles," he gasped.

Something clicked in Chrissy's brain. "We're in an old mine! There was one on the map in the newspaper clippings."

Alf took a piece of chalk from his pocket and drew arrows along the wall at regular intervals. "I hope we don't meet any ghosts down here," he said after a while. He tried to make it sound like a joke.

"If this was where X marked the spot and where the cat meant to lead us, maybe we're supposed to come face-to-face with some ghosts about now," Chrissy suggested. She looked out for the strange beast's glowing eyes somewhere in the darkness.

The deeper into the mine they went, the more stale the air and the more eerie their surroundings became. They reached the end of the tunnel and found themselves in a vast cavern. Both of the twins had the unsettling feeling that they were being watched. Alf felt a lump in his throat as he held up his green lantern to illuminate the velvet blackness. A thousand eyes glinted back at them.

Rockfall

"They're only bats," said Chrissy, squinting into the inky darkness. "Nothing to worry about. They're probably more frightened of us than we are of them."

"Who said I was worried?" said Alf.

"You look a bit green, that's all," Chrissy grinned.

"It's the light," said Alf. "I just hope that they're ordinary bats." He eyed them nervously, thinking of the weird cat and the huge brown moth. "Let's keep moving."

The twins crossed the cavern and discovered the entrances to two tunnels hewn into the solid rock wall. They didn't have the cat to lead the way, and no mysterious voices whispered to them. They had to decide which one to take. They picked the tunnel on the left.

Chrissy went first, her red lantern casting eerie shadows on the underground

passageway. The air was hot and stale and there was a strange rumbling sound somewhere up ahead in the darkness. Oh no, thought Alf. It's the ghost train.

"There's no turning back now," Chrissy shouted above the noise.

Suddenly, the walls of the tunnel began to shake violently, and pieces of rock and soil fell from the roof. The twins felt the ground rumble beneath them. They did their best to steady themselves.

Out of the corner of his eye, Alf saw something move above him, "Watch out!" he warned as a chunk of rock the size of a melon smashed the lantern from his grasp.

A cloud of dust came swirling toward the twins and they coughed and spluttered in the confusion. "I can't breathe," Chrissy choked, holding her hand up to her face.

The cloud was caused by part of a wall collapsing farther up the tunnel. One of the enormous wooden props holding up the roof began to groan under the weight of the thousands of tons of earth and rock above it. It sounded like the unearthly moans of some dying giant.

I don't like the sound of this. Let's get out of here!

The groaning stopped when the prop snapped in half and fell to the ground with a deafening CRASH. A few feet ahead of the twins, the roof started to cave in. The earth seemed to shift beneath them and both Alf and Chrissy lost their balance and fell to the ground.

Chrissy scrambled to her feet. "We've got to go back!" she yelled. "This whole place is going to come down on us."

The twins turned and ran back the way they'd come, but it was too late. Their path was blocked off by a freshly-fallen pile of rocks. "We're trapped," cried Alf, as another cloud of dust billowed toward them.

Confession from a Mystic

"I knew we shouldn't have trusted that cat and followed it here," said Chrissy, rubbing her elbow which felt a bit bruised. The rumbling had stopped when the last rock had fallen, and now the dust was beginning to settle.

"This mine can't have been used for ages," said Alf. "We're going to have to try to dig our way out if there's no other way." They hadn't thought to pack a shovel in their backpacks. "Let's look around."

They had only been exploring for a minute or two when they made a discovery. The rockfall had opened up a hole in one of the walls, leading to the other tunnel. Alf climbed through it without a moment's hesitation, and immediately tripped over something. "Careful," warned Chrissy and hurried across with the lantern. She held it up to reveal her brother sprawled over a pile of . . . bones. It was a skeleton.

Alf leaped to his feet. The skeleton was wearing a few dusty rags that must once have been a man's clothes. In his bony hand was a book.

Alf gulped and pried the book from the skeleton's fingers. He opened it. Chrissy stood beside him, holding up the lantern casting a red light on the yellowing pages.

To Whomsoever Shall Find Me

This is an account of my actions on the night of Tuesday last and I, Marcus Hillcutty pray that I shall not solely be judged a bad man. My intentions were good.

Myself

1

As the most celebrated passenger aboard the 7:15 train to Thurhorn I was invited by the driver of the locomotive (a Mr Stevens) to stand with him upon the footplate of 'The Gypsy Bell'.

2

I was, therefore, with him when we began to cross the bridge over the river Thur and together we witnessed it collapsing before our very eyes. Using my mystic powers, learned after many years of study, I muttered an incantation to save the train and all on board from a terrible fate.

3

I sent the train to Limbo in a matter of seconds. It is not a place in the same way that Seabry is a place. Limbo is nowhere. It is a place out of time. My plan was somehow to bring back the train when the danger of the storm and the broken bridge had passed.

4

Unfortunately, I fell from the speeding locomotive moments before it disappeared and I crawled, wounded, to the safety of this mine. I know that I shall not recover from my injuries, but it is the others I feel for.

5

I have condemned the passengers and crew to a fate worse than death. Oh, Now they must ride on an endless journey until the end of time itself. They never grow so much as a day older, but feel every second passing by on their neverending train ride to nowhere. Forgive

Alf turned the page once more. There was no writing on the next page. The rest of the book was blank.

The Search for Daylight

At last the twins understood why the mystic forces had wanted them to go to the abandoned mine ever since they had arrived in Seabry. If what Marcus Hillcutty had written in his notebook was true, and not the rantings of a dying man, the people on the ghost train were not ghosts at all. They were alive, but trapped out of time and in need of help. What didn't make sense to Alf and Chrissy was why *they* had been asked to help.

A sense of urgency suddenly swept over them. They had to get out of the mine fast. There was only one way to go, and that was to follow the tunnel that wasn't blocked off. After what seemed hours, they spotted daylight streaming through an opening, and a blast of fresh air smelling of . . . the sea! Alf and Chrissy scrambled up a pile of rocks and crawled through the gap onto a hillside.

Far below them stood Thurhorn Bridge, still bearing the scars of the storm of over eighty years before. Chrissy tried to imagine Marcus Hillcutty on the footplate of *The Gypsy Bell,* calling out an incantation in a desperate bid to save the train from steaming off the end . . . and condemning the passengers and crew to a timeless journey to nowhere.

Before either of them had time to fully take in their new surroundings, the twins' heads began to spin. Alf and Chrissy swayed dangerously from side to side. They were hundreds of feet up, which was why, way below, the River Thur looked like a harmless ribbon of blue.

"I think I'm going to fall!" screamed Alf.

"What's happening?" cried Chrissy. She shut her eyes tight to try to stop her head from spinning. When she opened them again, she found that she and Alf were no longer on the hillside.

Alf looked around in horror and amazement. "We're on the ghost train somewhere in Hillcutty's Limbo," he whispered in horror and amazement. "If what he wrote was true, we're out of time and place."

They stood in a compartment beside two men who sat playing a card game. Every inch of every wall seemed to be covered in pencil marks. Then the truth dawned on the twins. These men must have been playing cards for over eighty years, but probably looked as young as the day they stepped on board.

One of the players smiled triumphantly and laid down his cards. "I win," he said and leaned back to make a mark on the floor with a pencil. Then Alf and Chrissy realized the awful truth. Unless the twins could somehow help these

men, and everyone on board this doomed train, they would go on playing cards until the end of time . . . and would still keep score.

In another compartment, there sat a young woman. Chrissy found it almost impossible to believe that she must have been born over eighty years before.

If she hadn't been on a train whisked out of natural time by Marcus Hillcutty's misuse of unearthly powers, what would the woman have looked like? Would her hair have grown down to her waist and turned white long ago? Here it was as short and brown as the day she climbed aboard. The woman turned toward the twins, but did not seem to notice them.

The Truth is Told

Please help us.

Suddenly the scene changed, and Alf and Chrissy found themselves standing by a boy with his back to them. He was staring out of a window.

"I know you can hear me, Harold," he said. "Please help us. Send us the Alf and Chrissy you think about. Perhaps they are our only hope . . ."

The twins knew at once who they were watching. It was Bill Masters, Harold's twin brother. It seemed hard to believe that the boy was really the same age as old Harold Masters.

Alf and Chrissy's heads spun once more, and they found that they had returned to the hillside. Perhaps they had never actually left it. They were lying in the grass with Uncle Jack standing over them. He looked worried.

"Are you hurt?" he asked, concerned. "I knew it would come to this." They followed their uncle down the hillside to where he'd parked his car. "You'd better tell me exactly what you've been up to," he added, as they climbed into the back seat.

The twins decided that it was time to share their secret with someone. Everything seemed to be getting out of control. Who knew where it might lead them next? They had to take a chance and trust their uncle. On the way back to his home, they told him what had happened since they'd arrived in Seabry.

I think you have some explaining to do.

We know you're going to find this hard to believe, Uncle Jack...

Uncle Jack was a very good listener and didn't interrupt with a lot of stupid questions. By the time they returned to the station, they had finished their incredible story.

He walked through the front door and straight over to the bookshelf between the Left Luggage and Ticket offices. Above it hung a framed black and white photograph.

"You say that the big black cat you followed has only one ear?" he asked. The twins nodded. "Is this the one you saw?" He pointed to a cat in the photograph.

"That's it all right," said Alf. "But now it has amazing eyes ."

Their uncle took the photograph down from the wall and turned it over. "Read what it says on the back," he said. Alf and Chrissy read the words written in faded ink. "Arthur Bolt was Seabry's very last station master," he explained.

ARTHUR BOLT
and
CRUMBLE
(aged 10)

"His cat Crumble used to travel on the trains passing through here. She was on board the fateful 7:15 that tragic and stormy night. She must be over ninety years old now."

Alf suddenly realized what this meant. If Crumble had managed to return from *The Gypsy Bell* in Limbo, then it might be possible for the people on board to do the same. "If only we could find a way to help the poor passengers and crew," he said.

"If anyone can, you two can," said Uncle Jack mysteriously. "I think it's time I told you something about yourselves." He began to tell a strange tale . . .

The Power Behind The Beards

A hundred years ago, a group of people set up 'The Society For Men With Impressive Beards', and met in Thurhorn once a year.

A most impressive beard, sir.

And the same to you, sir.

To the outside world, they seemed a bunch of fools.

It's ridiculous! Grown men sitting around showing off their beards to each other.

In fact, the beards were just a front. These were some of the greatest minds of the day meeting in secret. Most of their beards were false. Some of the so-called bearded men were even women...

Is that you hiding behind that thing, Miss Johnson?

The president of the society was Marcus Hillcutty. Many people thought that his mystic magic was fake. We know that it was genuine.

The members of the society were working on a way to develop the power of the human mind...

I am raising this object using the power of thought alone.

Your great-grandmother was a member of the society and developed that power. She passed it on from generation to generation. You have these special powers. You were born with them.

Alf and Chrissy were dumbstruck. They didn't feel that they had any special powers!

"You have, but you haven't been shown how to use them yet," said Uncle Jack. "They're there, buried deep inside you. You've seen their effects already. It was your minds that made the window crack to show you the route of the old track . . . and made the moth appear just as you were wondering where you were supposed to go. What you . have to do now is to learn to control this power to put right a wrong. Hillcutty misused his powers, even though he was trying to help. He broke the laws of Nature. By taking the ghost train out of time, he changed the natural order of things. In fact, he changed history. Your job will be to try to put things back as they should have been before Hillcutty interfered. If you can do that, you'll be creating a new beginning for us all. We'll all be living the lives we would have led if the mystic hadn't messed things up."

"Wow!" gasped Alf. "You mean we could change history?"

"No, that would be dangerous. It was Hillcutty who changed the course of history. You will be trying to put things back as they should be. You will not only be trying to put the ghost train back on the right rails, but also time itself," said Uncle Jack. "I have been watching you ever since you arrived, waiting for the right time to reveal these secrets to you. You are twins, and often share feelings and thoughts. The people on the train were able to tap into the combined power of your minds."

I too have some of the powers developed by your great-grandmother . . . but, as twins, yours are twice the strength.

91

Using the Power

Uncle Jack explained the power developed by 'The Society For Men With Impressive Beards' to the twins. This was the power of thought, which their great-grandmother had helped to control. There was no spoon bending or tomfoolery. Under his watchful eye, Alf and Chrissy very quickly learned how to use it.

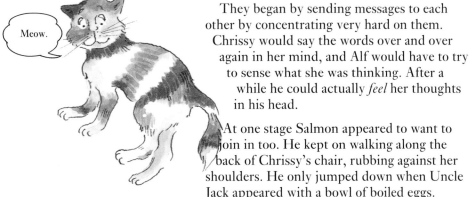

Meow.

They began by sending messages to each other by concentrating very hard on them. Chrissy would say the words over and over again in her mind, and Alf would have to try to sense what she was thinking. After a while he could actually *feel* her thoughts in his head.

At one stage Salmon appeared to want to join in too. He kept on walking along the back of Chrissy's chair, rubbing against her shoulders. He only jumped down when Uncle Jack appeared with a bowl of boiled eggs.

After supper, Alf swapped roles with Chrissy. This time he did the thinking, and she had to picture what was in his mind.

I don't understand this one.

I'm saying it's time you changed your socks!

Before bed, their uncle congratulated them on their progress. "Tomorrow you must put the power to a very important use," he reminded them. "You must *think* the train into stopping." Salmon interrupted with a purr. "Once you have broken its endless journey, it should become a solid train once more, and enter real time at exactly the moment Marcus Hillcutty made it disappear all those years ago," Uncle Jack went on. "That means it won't go over the end of the bridge . . . But that's tomorrow's task. What you need now is a good night's sleep."

The next morning, all three of them were up early. The sun was still low in the sky and the grass wet with dew as they made their way through the woods. They reached the tunnel, took a deep breath and stepped into the gloom.

Now the twins had to try to summon the train simply by concentrating on it. There was a sudden screech of metal wheels on the track. The train thundered out of nowhere and steamed at breakneck speed toward Alf and Chrissy who stood their ground on the track. The driver frantically pulled on his steam whistle and it hooted its warning like some monstrous owl.

Alf and Chrissy didn't move. They tried to think the train into stopping and becoming a normal solid machine again. They had to return it to that stormy night over eighty years before, which was its rightful place in time. It was working! Seconds before it reached them, *The Gypsy Bell* became a solid object as they had planned . . . BUT IT DID NOT STOP.

The twins managed to leap into an alcove in the wall. They just missed being crushed under the solid pounding wheels of the steam train before it disappeared back in time to the dreadful storm.

"Oh no!" screamed Chrissy. "We've put history right, but killed them all! What sort of a new beginning is this?" Everything went black.

A New Beginning

Chrissy blinked. Alf blinked. They couldn't believe their eyes. They were no longer in the tunnel but were standing next to Uncle Jack in brilliant sunlight. He was lifting some luggage out of his car. "You'll like Seabry," he was saying. "There will be plenty to do while you're here."

In front of them was a house the twins had never seen before. Standing in the doorway was Harold Masters and  another old man exactly like him. Alf and Chrissy couldn't tell them apart. "These are my friends Bill and Harold Masters," said their uncle. Then Alf and Chrissy understood . . . They had succeeded in changing history back to how it should have been!

Chrissy tried to remember what Uncle Jack had said would happen if they set time back on its rails. *"We'll all be living the lives we would have led if the mystic hadn't messed things up."* That was it. Everyone was now living in a new present . . . a present where they'd never met Harold Masters before! But how come Bill Masters was standing there, larger than life?

Alf was wondering the same thing. If they had sent the train back in time without stopping it, surely Bill Masters and all the other people on board must have hurtled off the end of the storm-wrecked bridge?

"We live over in Briary Manor," said Bill Masters, interrupting their thoughts. "We're having a party there on Sunday. Why not come over with your uncle? It's a double celebration."

"Yes," said Harold Masters. "Seabry has won the Best Kept Village Pond Competition again, and one of our local heroes is celebrating his one-hundred-and-tenth birthday. Here." He handed them a newspaper clipping. "This article from our local paper tells you all about him."

FREE BEARD TRIM AT MONICA'S

Simply bring this coupon to Monica's Salon and you're entitled to a thorough and professional beard trim free of charge.

This offer, to celebrate the salon's long association with The Society For Men With Impressive Beards, is only open to people with beards.

Haircuts are not offered as an alternative.

Alf and Chrissy read the clipping. They frowned and looked at each other. They reread the clipping. What did a free beard trim coupon have to do with saving lives? "I'm so sorry," said the old man. "I gave you the wrong clipping. Here's the one I meant you to read . . ."

'Safety Stevens' 110 this week

Samuel Stevens celebrates his 110th birthday this Friday. Better known as the engine driver Safety Stevens, he is famous for having saved the lives of all those on board the now infamous 7:15 to Thurhorn over eighty years ago.

When driving the train across Thurhorn Bridge in a terrible storm, he saw that part of the bridge had been washed away by the swollen river.

Unable to stop the train in time, he managed to disconnect his locomotive, *The Gypsy Bell*, from the rest of the train.

He, and those on board the footplate, then jumped clear.

The locomotive fell from the bridge into the raging waters below but the carriages stopped before reaching the edge.

Thanks to Safety Stevens's quick thinking, no one was killed and there was only one injury. Marcus Hillcutty, a famous mystic of the time, grazed his knee when jumping from the train. He had been riding alongside Safety Stevens on *The Gypsy Bell*.

That certainly explains why Bill Masters is alive and well, Alf thought when he had read the story. But why doesn't anyone else remember the other past?

"Probably because they don't have our combined powers," said Chrissy's voice inside his head.

Chrissy felt Salmon rubbing against her ankles. "That's funny," said Uncle Jack. "He's not usually that friendly with people he's never met before." Chrissy smiled to herself. Perhaps she and Alf weren't the only ones to remember their other past life after all . . . Perhaps Salmon also had some strange memory of the time when they had saved the ghost train to nowhere.

Did You Spot?

You can use this page to help spot things that could be useful in solving the mystery. First, there are hints and clues you can read as you go along. They will give you some idea what to look out for. Then there are extra notes to read which tell you more about what happened afterwards.

Hints and Clues

51 It isn't necessarily an owl. What else could it be?

52-53 Those ornaments and pictures are worth studying. And there may be more to that crack than at first meets the eye.

54-55 Smoke? Chrissy's theory isn't the only possibility.

56-57 Is someone - or something - watching them in the woods? Look closely.

58-59 Chrissy and Alf are twins and Harold Masters is also a twin. That's worth remembering.

60-61 Earthly train? Does Harold Masters know more than he's telling?

62-63 Take a close look at the whistle Alf has found.

64-65 A cat with one ear? Does it look at all familiar?

66-67 What's that by the plant on the shelf? A disguise? If so, what's it for? You may find out later.

68-69 It's important to study the names of the crew carefully. Something could fall into place. Seemingly silly things could turn out to be very important too.

70-71 You should know who the whistle belonged to by now, but don't jump to conclusions.

72-73 Can you name any of the people you can see aboard the train?

74-75 How did Harold Masters 'happen to be there' to find them? Was he just passing?

76-77 Things seem to be happening just when Chrissy and Alf want them to . . . Interesting.

78-79 Where can Chrissy have gone? What about checking the map in the newspaper clippings you saw earlier?

80-81 Not all those pairs of eyes are the same. It might be worth taking a closer look at the cavern . . .

84-85 Isn't that an old top hat in the shadows? Wasn't someone wearing one like that in an old photograph? The notebook explains a great deal. Read it with care!

86-87 On board the train, the people and compartments seem solid not ghost like.

88-89 So Uncle Jack admits to having been watching the twins . . .

90-91 You should know who the fake beard on the bookcase belonged to by now.

92-93 Carefully examine the train going over the edge of the bridge.

94-95 This really is a new beginning, isn't it? It's as though Alf and Chrissy's adventure never happened.

In the End

Now that the past has been changed back to how it should have been did you notice these changes in the present?

. . . Uncle Jack doesn't live in Seabry Station. (In fact, the bridge was repaired and the trains still run from Seabry to Thurhorn.)

. . . Harold Masters lives in Briary Manor, the home he grew up in. His parents had no reason to sell the house and go abroad because they didn't lose Bill.

. . . Seabry isn't a village of lost hope. According to the local paper, it has won the Best Kept Village Pond Competition on more than one occasion.

. . . The Society For Men With Impressive Beards is still going strong. (Who knows, you might even have bumped into a member without knowing it.)

. . . Uncle Jack doesn't remember anything about the twins adventure because his powers aren't as strong as theirs.

By the Way . . .

Did you spot:

. . . The silver whistle Alf found must have looked new as long as it was on the train. Once it was in 'real time' it began to age eighty years.

. . . The initials HM on the whistle stood for Henry Moose the guard on the train (mentioned on page 69), not Harold Masters.

. . . Marcus Hillcutty had sent the Akimbo diamond into Limbo, and he couldn't get that back either!

. . . It was the twins' great-grandmother's fake beard on Uncle Jack's bookcase.

96

HOUSE
OF SHADOWS

Karen Dolby

Illustrated by
Adrienne Kern

Contents

The Telegram

Ned and Kit Light were packing when the mysterious envelope arrived. Tomorrow they were moving to another house in another town, a long way away. Kit spotted the strange foreign stamp at once, then she read the words 'For the urgent attention of the Light Family' and ripped it open.

URGENT TELEGRAM

AN IMPORTANT MATTER CONCERNING A LOST ANCESTOR AND A SURPRISE INHERITANCE HAS COME TO LIGHT IN MYTHIKA. YOUR ASSISTANCE IS URGENTLY REQUIRED. PLEASE TRAVEL TO MYTHIKA AT ONCE FOR FURTHER DETAILS. PLANE TICKETS ENCLOSED FOR MR. AND MRS. TOM LIGHT. SPEED ESSENTIAL.

FROM MARCUS DALLY, LAWYER, ON BEHALF OF DEPARTMENT OF LOOSE ENDS, MYTHIKA.

FAST FORWARD AIRLINES INC.

Light / Mr. Thomas
Light / Mrs. Connie

DATE
September 10th

TIME
3:30pm

OPEN RETURN

FROM
Grand Central Airport

TO
Mythika

Look at the date on the ticket – it's tomorrow, the day of the move . . .

So Mum and Dad will be jetting off to Mythika while we're moving into the new house . . . alone.

The Day of the Move

The Shiftitkwik Removals' van screeched to a halt outside Number 1, Spectral Lane, an old house standing all alone at the end of a long, narrow road on the outskirts of a small town called Hallows-on-the-Hill. The Light family followed close behind in their car and found Mr. Grey, the leasing agent, waiting impatiently outside the front gates.

That van driver is a lunatic – I'll be surprised if anything's still in one piece.

Ned and Bullseye, the dog, peered up at their new home. Dark, diamond-shaped windows stared back at them. Weeds sprouted in the drive and tall iron gates leaned crazily against the crumbling walls. A decaying sign, half hidden by weeds still hung from one gate. "Hallows Grange, to Rent" it said. Meanwhile, Mr. Light signed the grubby documents that Mr. Grey flung at him and Mrs. Light checked the road map for their route to the airport.

100

Kit stared open-mouthed as their belongings whizzed past and disappeared into the dark interior of the house. Promising to send the bill, the removals' men waved and disappeared in a cloud of exhaust fumes. Mr. Grey sped away in the opposite direction.

Ned and Kit were left feeling slightly dazed as they said goodbye to their parents and tried hard to sound cheerful. Both thought about their parents' mysterious mission. What would they find in Mythika? Who was their lost ancestor . . . and what was the surprise inheritance?

They waved until the car was out of sight and then turned to the house. Suddenly, as if from nowhere, a short, very old man appeared. Smiling, he walked up to them.

"So, you're moving in . . . into the house of shadows," he said, pointing to the house. He paused, then added so softly they could hardly hear, "You might be the ones . . . they've been waiting."

"What do you mean?" Kit asked, "Don't go . . ." but the man turned away, vanishing into a thick mist which suddenly swirled around them. Kit glanced at Ned, who shrugged and tapped his head.

"Nuts," he said. "Come on, let's go inside."

Hallows Grange

Inside, the house was damp and chilly. Kit shivered in spite of the warm day outside. "The house of shadows," she muttered, staring out of the window. "The name suits it."

"Look what I've found," Ned grinned, after rummaging through one of the boxes. "Food! This will cheer us up."

Crunching chocolate chip cookies, they began to explore. They drew back curtains and threw open the windows, but the house remained gloomy and cold. Ned looked wistfully out at the sunny garden.

The old house was strangely silent and their footsteps echoed as they walked through rooms filled with odd, old fashioned furniture. Kit stared at the pictures on the walls, wondering who had lived here before, when a clock began to chime. Ned and Kit both jumped at the sound and it was then that they heard a faint tick tock, tick tock, growing slowly but surely louder and faster.

"It's as if the house is slowly coming back to life," said Ned, thoughtfully.

Kit wanted the attic room as her bedroom. She liked the sloping, beamed ceiling and the comfy brass bed. She lugged her bulging suitcase up the narrow, rickety staircase, but as she reached the top, flickering shadows skipped across the ceiling.

The little room was icily cold. Kit shivered. Then a sudden noise made her turn and she froze, rooted to the spot, as a radio lying on the bed crackled to life. Kit knew that she hadn't switched it on.

Ki.i.i.i.t.t.
He.e.e.e.e.l.p.

Suddenly, the attic didn't seem such a good idea. Bumping her suitcase behind her, she scooted downstairs, almost tripping over Bullseye who was growling at . . . at nothing.

Kit bent down and patted the dog. She glanced up just in time to see a fleeting shadow which for an instant looked like a young girl. But that was impossible. She shrugged and laughed nervously, "First I hear things, now I'm seeing things. This old house is giving me the creeps."

Soon, all was forgotten as Kit and Ned munched their way through a huge supper of beans, toast and chocolate, in front of a roaring fire. But Ned had the uncomfortable feeling he was being watched and Bullseye prowled the room sniffing uneasily. Suddenly the lights dimmed, then flared brightly, the curtains billowed and an owl hooted. At the edges of the room the shadows gathered and a thin white mist filled the air.

A Strange Scene

Kit and Ned stared unbelievingly as the swirling mist grew so dense they could hardly see. The air was filled with a strange, choking smell, like smoke and their heads spun dizzily. Then, as swiftly as the mist had come, it disappeared and the air was clear.

Kit looked around in confusion. They were sitting in a different room. Or were they? The furniture was new, bright sunlight shone through an open window and an unknown dog lay on the rug in front of them. But there was something very familiar about the layout of the room . . .

Ned ran to the window. "This is incredible," he said, as he began to climb out. Kit looked out in amazement, then followed him.

"It's like a film set," Kit croaked, when she finally found her voice. She paused. "Or as if we've been transported back in time."

No one took any notice of Ned or Kit, or even seemed to see them. Kit jumped out of the way as a small boy chasing a pig headed straight for her. She had the weird idea that he would simply have run on through her, as if she wasn't there. It was almost as though they were invisible.

"Look at the house!" cried Ned, turning suddenly. "It's grown." They gazed back in disbelief. Their house was recognizable, but it formed just a small side wing of a larger, more impressive stone building. What had happened? Kit was struggling to make sense of it all when the huge oak doors of the big house were flung open.

A tall, sinister figure, in a long flowing coat stepped out and stood framed by the doorway. Was it Ned's imagination or did everyone pause and shrink back? Kit and Ned looked on in silence as a scene unfolded in front of their eyes, like an act from a play. As they watched, the players seemed to move in slow motion as if the scene was often rehearsed and repeated. Kit had a strange feeling that she had heard the words before.

A young girl pleaded with the man in the long flowing coat. "Please Mr. Hubble, don't take my brother away."

Mr. Hubble ignored the girl and marched briskly to a waiting carriage. He was followed by a pale faced boy who looked about the same age as Ned. Mr. Hubble waited impatiently, looking at no one, while the boy's mother and sister said a tearful goodbye, then he grasped the boy roughly by the arm and pulled him inside.

From the window of the carriage, Mr. Hubble stared back at the house. His piercing eyes looked straight through the spot where Ned and Kit were standing. Kit shivered as the man smiled, not warmly, but with a cold, evil grimace. The carriage rumbled away along the cobbled track and the boy's mother stood crying, whispering to herself, "I know I shall never see him again . . ."

As Ned and Kit looked on, a chilling mist appeared as if from nowhere, shrouding the house and swallowing everyone around it. Their heads began to spin and the scene faded . . .

Night Falls

They were back where they had started, sitting in front of the roaring fire. Ned and Kit turned to one another. What was going on? What had they witnessed – a scene from the past? Was it possible? Suddenly Kit yawned, all she wanted was to go to sleep. Ned felt tired too, so tired that he could hardly keep his eyes open. It was late and perhaps things would make more sense tomorrow. The house could wait till the morning . . . But the house, or something in it, had other ideas.

Ned opened his bedroom door. He shivered. Something strange was going on. What was that peculiar feeling? It was almost as if . . . as if he was waiting for something to happen. Trying hard to ignore it, he climbed into his new bed. He tossed and he turned but it was no good. He was wide awake now. Perhaps it was because of the moonlight streaming into the room through the uncurtained windows. Perhaps . . .

Suddenly Ned sat upright in bed and as if obeying a secret voice, he stared at the ornate mirror standing on the chest of drawers opposite. At first the mirror was a gleaming blank. It reflected nothing. Then, with a shock, Ned saw a different room in the glass. Lit by sunlight, it was still his room, but furnished as it would have been years, maybe centuries before.

He gasped as he saw a face reflected in the glass. It was like his own, but not his. It was the face of the boy they had seen earlier with the sinister Mr. Hubble. He looked pale and ghostly and stared at Ned as if he could see him . . . as if he wanted his help. Then the boy turned to the door and Ned heard the faint sound of someone crying.

Meanwhile, Kit was sleeping peacefully with Bullseye lying happily across her feet. Her new bed felt warm and snug and she had quickly forgotten the strange experiences of the day. Instead she was dreaming of imaginary adventures in sunny Mythika, of her parents on their mysterious mission, of a surprise inheritance and an endless supply of enormous strawberry ice cream sundaes that were almost too big to eat . . .

Her dream didn't last long, however, and Kit reluctantly returned to Hallows Grange. She woke with a start to the sound of angry voices.

Kit blinked in the darkness, feeling sleepy and confused. She stared in disbelief at two ghostly figures who were arguing angrily at the foot of her bed.

"Never!" the girl's voice screamed.

Moonlight flooded the room and Kit saw the girl's face clearly for the first time – she was the sister of the pale faced boy in the strange scene from the past.

The ghosts, or whatever they were, seemed to become more solid and real in front of her eyes as her own room grew fainter.

"I'll never agree!" the girl shouted, racing from the room, closely followed by Mr. Hubble.

They seemed to run straight through the wall, but when Kit looked again, she saw the outline of a door emerging and growing solid. Kit could make no sense of what was happening, but she knew she should follow the girl. She slipped out of bed and tiptoed to the door that had just appeared in the wall. Slowly she turned the handle.

House of Shadows

The door opened and Kit stepped out of the room. She gasped in amazement. An apparently endless corridor stretched in front of her, lined with the sort of pictures and furniture she had only seen in museums. She was in a different house . . . or was she? Then she remembered the strange scene they had witnessed earlier and the answer became clear. Long ago their home had once been part of a much bigger house and she was now inside it.

A shiver ran down her spine. Was it fear or excitement? Kit couldn't tell. She began to walk, almost as though she were dreaming and would wake at any moment, yet she had the curious feeling she was being led somewhere, or was looking for something.

She stopped with a jolt. As she stared into a gold-edged mirror, she saw . . . nothing! There was a hazy glow, but she had no reflection. She stepped back and sideways and shook her head, but still saw only the wall behind her. What was happening?

"I'm a ghost here," she whispered, shuddering. Suddenly, all she wanted to do was go back to bed and wake up in her own home in her own time, but something made her go on.

Candles burned brightly in their holders along the corridor. The flickering light sent shadows playing across the ceiling and walls. She marched bravely on and, turning a corner, saw a heavy red curtain moving. Had someone brushed against it recently? Kit looked again and realized that it was drawn across the entrance to another passage. She slipped through and shivered as an icy blast of air whistled around her. The curtain billowed out behind her.

"I don't want to walk along here," she thought.

Was it her imagination, or did someone really hiss in reply, "You must. Hurry!"

Kit began to walk quickly, faster and faster until she was running. As she ran, Kit became aware of someone crying. Where was the sound coming from? Ahead or behind? It seemed to be everywhere.

Kit ran up and down stairs, opened doors and stared into deserted rooms. As each door opened, she hoped to reach the end of her search. On and on she raced, but still the crying continued. She was sure it was Catherine, the girl she had seen in her room.

The crying was as loud as ever, leading Kit further into the old house, yet she never seemed to get any closer. She saw no one but in each room she felt certain that someone had left only seconds before.

Breathless and confused, she finally stopped. In the shadows of a conservatory, half hidden by tropical plants, stood the grim figure of . . . Mr. Hubble. Slowly, he turned around. Kit gulped. Everything went black.

A Spooky Message

Ned yawned and stretched. "I had the weirdest dream," he muttered to Bullseye, who had just slunk into the room.

He blinked and opened his eyes wide in surprise as he caught sight of the mirror opposite and read the thin, spidery letters written across the glass.

Meanwhile, Kit stirred in her sleep. Her bed felt strangely hard and lumpy. Awake, but with her eyes still shut, she realized she felt very cold, and something prickly was tickling her nose.

She opened one eye suspiciously. This was definitely NOT her bedroom. Where was she? She sat up quickly and found herself fighting her way through a huge and very spiky yucca plant.

"What am I doing here?" she spluttered, looking around at the ruins of the crumbling conservatory. She had been lying on an old stone bench.

The last thing she remembered was Mr. Hubble's sinister stare. Kit shivered at the thought of it.

"Ned won't believe this . . ." she muttered to herself, walking slowly back upstairs. Kit hardly believed what had happened herself.

Ten minutes later, Ned and Kit finished their stories. "We can't both just have been dreaming," said Kit, staring at the writing on Ned's mirror. "There's something very strange about this house. No wonder that old man called it the house of shadows."

Bullseye growled. Kit grabbed Ned's arm. "Look," she whispered, pointing through the open door. Ned stared and from the expression on his face, Kit knew he could also see . . .

A ghost! In the doorway stood a pale shadow of a young boy. As they watched, he turned to face them staring into their eyes with a sad, helpless expression. Neither was surprised to recognize the boy who had disappeared in the carriage with Mr. Hubble, the face Ned had seen reflected in the mirror.

"Don't go," Kit called hesitantly, but the shadowy figure began to fade, growing almost transparent before he vanished into the air.

Later, slurping hot chocolate and munching toast in the sunny garden, Ned and Kit tried to make sense of things. "I know we've been seeing ghosts," said Kit at last. "But I get the feeling it's the house that's haunting us, showing us snippets of what happened here in the past . . . something awful."

"But why?" asked Ned, not expecting an answer. "If only we knew more, like what happened to the big old house and who lived here. But how can we find out?"

Ned and Kit stared at one another and exclaimed together. "That weird old man!" He definitely seemed to know more than he said yesterday. And it was he who had first mentioned the house of shadows. He was their only lead. If they could find him, maybe he could explain.

111

Hallows-on-the-Hill

Ned looked at Kit. "Well?" he asked. "Come on. What are we waiting for? Let's go into the town and find him."

But Kit had already gone. Ned raced after her, struggling into his jacket as he ran. Bullseye frolicked around his feet, happy to be outside. Behind them the house watched, guarding its secret.

Hallows-on-the-Hill, as well as being farther away than it had looked, was also much bigger. In despair, Kit gazed around her at the bustling streets and shops. "Where do we start?" she asked, glumly.

Ned shrugged, then turned decisively down one of the busiest looking streets. Occasionally, someone looked at them curiously as if wondering who they were, but most people hurried by, intent on their own business. Kit began to wonder what they had hoped to find out here. There were certainly no clues leaping out at them.

"We'll have to find someone to ask about the house and the old man," she said, finally. A small grocery store seemed a good starting point.

Ned quickly chose a bar of Mango Melts and casually tried to question the shopkeeper. "Um . . . we've just moved into Hallows Grange and wondered if . . ." he stopped.

There was a shocked gasp. As if by magic, the crowded shop emptied. The shopkeeper shoved Ned's change at him and said abruptly, "We're closed." With that, Ned and Kit found themselves back outside.

112

Even more determined, they decided to try somewhere else. They chose a bustling cafe with a friendly looking owner and waitress. Perched on stools at the bar, Ned and Kit began again. This time, Ned decided not to say where they lived. He described the old man they had seen, aware of a prickly silence around the cafe. Then several people began talking at the same time.

Neither the cafe owner nor the waitress would say more. Kit and Ned were left feeling more confused than ever. They walked slowly on, heading for the old town walls in gloomy silence. It was very still and quiet when they heard a familiar voice.

"Ned, Kit – I believe you were looking for me," it said.

113

A Sorry Tale

Ned and Kit spun around to see . . . the old man. Ned felt cold shivers run down his spine as the man greeted them. How did he know their names? "Creepy!" he thought to himself. One look at Kit told him she felt like running away, too. But they had to stay. They wanted to find out about the house of shadows and Ned was more certain than ever that the man knew something.

"You've seen the house of shadows," the man said. "I knew you would."

Kit nodded. "How did you know?" she asked. "What do you mean?"

"My name is Amos Goodfellow and I shall tell you what I can," the old man replied. "Hallows Grange has been haunted for as long as anyone can remember. People have seen flickering shadows, heard whispered voices and felt icy hands touch their faces. Some have even seen the ghostly outline of the house of shadows – the big house from the past."

He paused and glanced at them before continuing his strange story, a tale so vivid that Kit and Ned could almost picture the scenes in their minds.

My name is Amos Goodfellow.

The house has been empty for a long time. People say it's too damp or too dark, but everyone knows those aren't the real reasons.

Long ago the house and all the land nearby was owned by the Golightly family. They were fair and respected landowners and the house was famous for its parties and hospitality.

Then disaster struck and the house changed hands under sinister circumstances. Mr. Hubble, the new squire, was cruel and miserly. Both he and the house seemed cursed and when half the house was destroyed by fire, there was no money left to rebuild.

Soon only the west wing remained – where you live now. The rest simply tumbled down out of neglect.

To Rent

A Shadowy Figure

K it turned to ask another question, but Amos had vanished as mysteriously as the first time they had seen him. "It all seems a bit far-fetched to me," she said. "And I don't know how much I trust that man. His disappearing trick is too convenient – he tells us just enough to keep us interested."

Kit and Ned scuffed their way home. They had learned something about the house, but most of their questions were unanswered.

As they walked through the gates of Hallows Grange, Kit stared hard at their house. A curtain moved and then twitched again. A shadowy figure darted out of sight. Someone, or something was in there. Kit suddenly felt very angry. "I'm sick of these tricks . . . If it's someone's idea of a joke, it isn't very funny. I want to know exactly what IS going on!" she yelled at Ned, who watched in amazement as Kit stormed up to the house. She flung open the front door and ran inside.

Ned arrived to find Kit in the kitchen, red in the face with embarrassment, and speechless. A friendly woman in an apron seemed to be emptying boxes and . . . he sniffed, cooking something delicious. Ned was still trying to decide precisely what was in the saucepan and wondering whether it could be for them, when he realized that he hadn't a clue who this woman was.

"I'm Tilda Daly," she said, before Ned asked. "Your parents asked me to help out while they're away."

After his third bowl of soup, followed by a mega helping of rhubarb crumble swimming in custard, Ned began to feel very comfortable and at home. He listened sleepily as Kit, now over her embarrassment, chatted to Tilda. He guessed she was trying to find out more about Hallows Grange.

"There have always been stories, of course," Tilda said. "Because it's an old house, people claim to have seen . . . things, you know. But you don't want to listen to that nonsense. I've never seen anything."

"Do you know anything about the history of the house and the people who used to live here?" Kit prompted.

"Hallows Grange has been empty for a long time now," Tilda said. "If you want to know anything about it, there's a whole stack of books and even some old photos and things which were left here. They're in a trunk in the attic, I seem to remember. And there are always the portraits – mind you, they're a funny-looking bunch."

Kit felt like kicking herself. Of course they should have looked at the portraits and she had even glanced at the trunk in the attic. The house itself was the obvious place to look for information. She was sure that the answer to all their questions was here and an eerie voice inside her head told her that the house itself wanted them to discover its secret.

In the Attic

They found the large trunk in the attic, bound with bands of metal and heavy brass clasps. Surprisingly, the chest was not locked. The lid creaked open to reveal a curious and amazing assortment of books, clothes, pictures and other mementoes. It looked as though it had not been disturbed for centuries. Kit delved in and began sorting through.

June 13th 1790

HMS MEDUSA SINKS NO SURVIVORS

The criminal transportation ship, The Medusa, has been lost off the coast of Mythika in heavy seas. Her captain, Carruthers Crook, has sailed the ship safely through these waters for more than 10 years. Captain Crook and his crew were lost with the ship. There were no survivors.

LAWRENCE'S

...E STARTS NOW!

...e boned corsets,

April 10th 1790

Jebediah Grimshaw

Are your instructions clear? I don't want to know the details, but Thomas must be separated from the others. There must be no doubt . . . I will pay you five guineas at the harbour when The Endeavour sails. The 30 guineas will be yours when you return . . . alone. The choice of crew is up to you.

Ebenezer Hubble

Ebenezer Hubble & son Gervase
anno 1788

The clock chimed the half hour, then the hour . . . and a second hour. The shadows lengthened, but Ned and Kit were too busy to notice. At first they just glanced at the old letters, notes and papers, feeling more than a little guilty, as if they were snooping. But curiosity and the overwhelming sense that they were meant to be there soon took over.

Shadows Gather

K it sighed as she finished reading. She felt that she still knew very little. The eerie voice in her head seemed to tell her it was all connected with Thomas Golightly's will and the sinister Mr. Hubble. She shivered. Was this why she and Ned were being haunted? Someone wanted their help – could it be to foil some dastardly plan plotted by the evil Hubble?

Kit noticed for the first time how dark the room was. Out of the corners of her eyes she could see the shadows gathering. She and Ned sat unable to move. The mist thickened and seemed to swirl around them. Their heads reeled as the room spun and they knew, even before the dense mist cleared, that they were now in another time . . . in shadow time.

They watched transfixed as a scene unfolded before their eyes. Just as before, when they first saw the house of shadows, it was as if they were watching an act from a play. But as the story emerged, they realized that the scenes were being played in reverse order.

The light faded, leaving Ned and Kit in the darkness, waiting for something they both knew would happen without knowing what it might be. The moon rose to reveal a study. The door slowly opened and Edward slipped silently into the room, unaware of the sinister figure lurking half hidden in the shadows behind a chair.

The figures disappeared. Kit and Ned now found themselves outside among some trees, blinking in the sunlight. Edward and Catherine were talking in hushed voices.

Kit had heard enough. She already knew what would happen. She ran to where Edward was standing. "Don't do it," she yelled. "It's a trap."

Ghosts from the Future

Kit grabbed Edward's arm and pleaded once more, "Don't take the money. It's a trap."

She knew it was useless. She had no way of making Catherine and Edward hear. Yet they seemed to sense something.

It seemed like a warning – but that's silly.

"How strange," said Edward, brushing her unseen hand away, "I felt an icy hand touch my arm."

"And did you hear something?" asked Catherine in an anxious voice. "Words I couldn't catch, a ghostly whispering."

The edges of the trees grew faint and blurred as the scene faded. Mist swirled and their heads spun. Once again Ned and Kit returned to their own time and the twilight of the attic.

"Edward could feel it when you touched him," Ned exclaimed. "It was as if you were the ghost."

"We WERE the ghosts," Kit replied slowly. "Ghosts from the future, being shown a glimpse of the past . . . It's as if a story is being told to us."

"But not in the right order," Ned added.

A house full of spooks and weird goings-on and this place scares you!

All these old things are giving me the creeps.

"I've just realized something," said Kit, almost whispering with fear. "Catherine and Edward . . . those are OUR real names."

"It could be a coincidence," Ned began. But he knew it was more than that. Some secret voice told him their own fate was somehow tied up with this brother and sister from so long ago. The idea made Ned feel cold and threatened. But part of him knew it was true.

"Let's go," said Ned, closing the trunk. "Nothing else is going to happen today."

As if in answer, the light flickered, growing suddenly bright and then dim. Ned and Kit blinked in the gloom as mist engulfed them. They were in the study again. Once more the door creaked open. This time, they watched Hubble creeping stealthily into the room with a sheet of parchment in his hand. He looked furtively around, took out a small gold key from his pocket, and then opened one of the desk drawers.

"What is he doing?" Kit whispered.

It was so dark it was hard to see much, but Hubble seemed to be looking for something. He paused and then pulled out a paper edged with a green border. He smiled as he tucked it swiftly inside his coat and carefully replaced it with the red edged parchment he had been carrying.

The room and Hubble grew pale and transparent. A thin mist filled the air and a familiar dizziness brought them swiftly back to the attic. Suddenly a small window blew open and a gust of wind howled around the room, lifting an ancient, faded newspaper from a wooden casket in the far corner. The wind died as suddenly as it had come, dropping the yellowing newspaper open at their feet. They began to read.

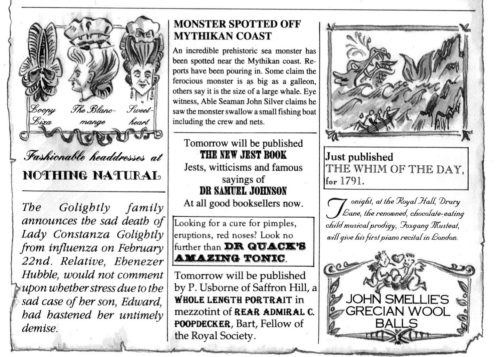

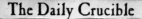

The Daily Crucible

LORD'S SON FOUND GUILTY OF THEFT

FRIDAY February 24th, 1790

Edward Golightly, son of the late Lord Thomas Golightly of All Hallows, today stood trial for theft. He was accused of stealing a purse full of gold coins from his father's cousin, Ebenezer Hubble, who is now in charge of the All Hallows estate. Edward's only sister, Catherine, was seen weeping in the courtroom.

Ebenezer Hubble is himself a judge, not noted for softness - he won last year's Judge Jefferies award for sending more prisoners to the gallows than any other judge. At yesterday's trial he was quoted as saying, "It saddens me to bring the boy to trial - he is my beloved cousin's son. But he had disgraced the family's reputation and shamed his father's name. Justice must be done, however painful."

Judge Hubert Stern, a former pupil of Mr Hubble's summed up by saying, "The overwhelming evidence against the boy leaves me no alternative but to sentence him to seven years' transportation to the colonies."

Many were shocked by the harshness of the punishment. Edward Golightly will sail on The Medusa, which leaves on March 30th.

Artist's drawing of Edward Golightly in the dock.

Fashionable headdresses at
NOTHING NATURAL

Loopy Liza *The Blanc-mange* *Sweet-heart*

The Golightly family announces the sad death of Lady Constanza Golightly from influenza on February 22nd. Relative, Ebenezer Hubble, would not comment upon whether stress due to the sad case of her son, Edward, had hastened her untimely demise.

MONSTER SPOTTED OFF MYTHIKAN COAST

An incredible prehistoric sea monster has been spotted near the Mythikan coast. Reports have been pouring in. Some claim the ferocious monster is as big as a galleon, others say it is the size of a large whale. Eye witness, Able Seaman John Silver claims he saw the monster swallow a small fishing boat including the crew and nets.

Tomorrow will be published
THE NEW JEST BOOK
Jests, witticisms and famous sayings of
DR SAMUEL JOHNSON
At all good booksellers now.

Looking for a cure for pimples, eruptions, red noses? Look no further than **DR QUACK'S AMAZING TONIC**.

Tomorrow will be published by P. Usborne of Saffron Hill, a **WHOLE LENGTH PORTRAIT** in mezzotint of **REAR ADMIRAL C. POOPDECKER**, Bart, Fellow of the Royal Society.

Just published
THE WHIM OF THE DAY,
for 1791.

Tonight, at the Royal Hall, Drury Lane, the renowned, chocolate-eating child musical prodigy, Foxgang Musteat, will give his first piano recital in London.

JOHN SMELLIE'S GRECIAN WOOL BALLS

Ned and Kit finished reading. They now knew the sad fates of both Edward and Mrs. Golightly.

"The Medusa!" Kit exclaimed, remembering the newspaper clipping they had found in the trunk. "That was the ship that sank," she sighed, feeling strangely stunned and surprised. "Poor Edward must have drowned."

As she spoke she glanced at the open wooden chest in the corner of the room, where the newspaper had come from. At the bottom lay a yellowed, but familiar-looking sheet of paper. Kit was amazed to find another will by Thomas Golightly, but this was different from the one they had already seen.

GOLIGHTVS FIAT LIGHTVS

Last Will and Testament of Thomas Golightly

I, Thomas Golightly, Lord Golightly of All Hallows, being of sound mind, leave my estate and title to my dear son, Edward. My beloved wife, Constanza, and daughter, Catherine, shall live on at Hallows Grange for as long as they wish. They will also receive an annual income (my solicitor, J. Doolittle, holds the details). I appoint my good friend, Amos Goodfellow, as adviser to Edward until Edward reaches the age of 21.

Signed: T. Golightly

Kit was puzzled. What did the two wills mean? She replaced the will and newspaper in the casket and closed the lid. Absent mindedly, she wiped away the thick layer of dust to reveal a shiny mahogany top. To her horror, she found herself gazing down at Ebenezer Hubble. He smiled his sinister smile. Kit's gasp broke the spell. As Ned, too, stared down, the image vanished.

The Story Unfolds

Kit and Ned walked back down the rickety attic stairs. "Things seem to be speeding up," said Kit.

"Perhaps we're building up to the climax of the final act," Ned said.

"I wonder why Thomas Golightly changed his will," Kit pondered. "And WHY did he leave Hubble in charge?"

"But DID he change his will?" asked Ned. "Hubble was switching papers in the study and the one he took away looked suspiciously like the will we've just seen. Suppose the other one leaving him in control is a forgery? I wonder what happened to Thomas Golightly?

As if in answer, the shadows grew solid and characters materialized, coming to life as yet another scene unfolded before Ned and Kit's eyes. A group of people stood gathered in a library. Kit recognized the familiar faces of Edward and Catherine, their mother and Mr. Hubble. The rest were strangers, but who was the old man – the spitting image of Amos Goodfellow?

Everyone looked very solemn as the man sitting at the desk placed a pair of spectacles carefully on his nose. He cleared his throat and began to read out the will of Thomas Golightly. As he did so, Kit knew with a peculiar certainty that this scene and the last were being shown in the correct order. But why? Could it be that whatever power was responsible for revealing these snatches of the past, was determined that the truth of Hubble's actions should not be lost or mistaken.

I, Solomon Doolittle, of Doolittle and Dally, now read the last will of Thomas Golightly. I appoint as my executor, my trusted and beloved cousin, Ebenezer Hubble . . .

A shocked gasp ran around the room. Amos started with surprise and looked alarmed while the others whispered anxiously together. Only Hubble looked unsurprised and smirked to himself.

The scene faded and changed. Kit and Ned were now looking at a group of familiar figures in the room. Suddenly Kit realized that the past was rewinding once more and this unhappy episode came before the reading of the will.

Thank you, Amos.

You know you can always rely on my help for anything.

Lost in the jungle the letter said . . . Perhaps there is still hope.

The message from Grimshaw, the guide, suggests the worst.

Naturally I hired the best guides and servants . . . The expediton should have been a great success.

The temperature dropped suddenly. Kit and Ned found themselves sitting on the steps of a bustling dockside. A ship was being loaded ready to sail. Edward, Catherine and Mrs. Golightly stood with a man Ned guessed was Thomas Golightly. Meanwhile, Hubble whispered furtively with a man they had never seen before. He seemed to be handing over a purse full of money.

God speed your return.

Goodbye Thomas.

I am paying you generously. You understand Grimshaw – there must be no doubt . . . Thomas must not come back.

Hubble's Diary

Kit and Ned were still shivering from the cold and damp when they felt the now familar spinning sensation. They found themselves back inside the house of shadows, alone . . . with the sinister Mr. Hubble.

"This is getting confusing," hissed Ned.

"There's no need to whisper, he can't . . ." Kit stopped.

Hubble spun around and stared blankly in their direction. He looked puzzled.

"No one there . . . I'm plagued by echoes," he muttered to himself. He took down a crimson, leather bound book from a shelf and, sitting at the desk, began to write.

> This is no time for remorse. I must speak to Catherine again about my son, Gervase.

Curiosity got the better of Kit. Stepping silently forward, she peered over Hubble's shoulder and quickly beckoned Ned. "It's his diary!" she almost exclaimed, remembering to whisper just in time.

September 1st 1791

Through my trickery, Edward is safely out of the way now, never to return to reclaim his inheritance. Hallows Grange is mine and yet ... at night when all is quiet I miss them - all of them, especially Thomas. He was my cousin and childhood friend - better than me at everything, always liked, master of Hallows Grange and my benefactor. I plotted against him when he planned that ridiculous botanical exploration trip. He was so excited about it all. I hired the phony guide and arranged to have him "lost". I switched wills, so a forgery was read out, giving me, at least temporarily, charge of the estate. But when the shadows gather, I am afraid — my guilt weighs heavily. Is it guilt which stops me destroying the real will?

But this is no time for remorse. What's done cannot be changed. Gervase must smarten himself up, make a better impression. If he and Catherine marry, the title and inheritance are secure. Lord Hubble of All Hallows. . . . . What's that? The shadowy spirits that haunt me are here again —

Ned and Kit were still reading when Hubble stood up suddenly, sending them flying to avoid him. He began to pace around the room talking aloud. Something told Kit and Ned that time had moved on from the other scenes. Hubble was now master of the house.

She WILL marry Gervase. The estate will then belong to the Hubbles forever. One way or another she must be persuaded.

This nonsense about not liking him. The boy has some admirable qualities, I'm sure. If only I could think of something . . .

Master. This letter has arrived for the late mistress, Constanza.

I'll take it.

Aah! It can't be! No one must ever know. All would be ruined.

Startling News

Both Ned and Kit were asking themselves the same question. Why had the letter shocked Hubble so much? Ned snatched at the paper as it fluttered down, catching it before it reached the floor. Eagerly, he and Kit began to read.

Mythika
August 5th 1791

Dear Madam,

You do not know me, but I was Midshipman on HMS Medusa. I wish you to know that your son, Edward, did not perish with the ship as thought. He is alive, though very weak and being cared for here in Mythika. He seems to have lost his memory and needs his family's help and support.

He and I were the sole survivors and I myself do not expect to survive my injuries. I am worried about your son. I came to know him well during the voyage and am convinced of his innocence of any crime. I could not rest easy knowing his plight so far from home.

Your obedient servant,
Samuel Tar

Kit nudged Ned. "He looks as if he's seen a ghost."

That was exactly what Hubble thought he was seeing, or not seeing. He stared in horror at the letter which looked as if it was floating in mid-air.

"I'm doomed!" he wailed. "I hear voices whispering in my ear and now spirits, sent to haunt me forever." He paused and then in a different, crafty tone spoke aloud to the room. "This changes nothing. My plans will succeed and Edward can rot in Mythika. No one will ever know he is alive."

You don't frighten me. I can't see you, but I know you're there.

With that, he stormed from the room. Everything blurred and grew misty. When Kit and Ned could see again they were back in their own time. Kit slumped into the nearest armchair. It was hard to keep up with events. The more they found out about Ebenezer Hubble, the more evil he seemed.

"But why are we being shown all this?" puzzled Ned feeling exhausted. "What are we supposed to do?"

There is no doubt. She drowned last night. We found the poor girl's hat, but the lake is so deep we may never find her body . . .

Foolish girl! This is your fault, Gervase . . . This displeases me.

"They're talking about Catherine," exclaimed Ned, as the picture faded. "She must have drowned after poor Edward was sent away."

Kit jumped at the sudden noise as the telephone rang. It was their mother speaking from a long distance, but it was a bad line and the phone went dead before she had finished. Kit stared wondering at the receiver. "The name . . . the Golightlys must be our ancestors," she gasped at last. "We HAVE to save Catherine and tell her Edward didn't drown. NOW I'm certain our lives are linked to theirs." A silent voice seemed to whisper that this was their mission.

"I think we'll know when the time comes," Kit replied.

The door creaked open. Kit and Ned stared expectantly, but it was only Bullseye. He sniffed the air suspiciously, growling as the fur rose on his neck. All at once the television flickered to life and three figures appeared on the screen – Hubble, his son Gervase and Amos!

Sorry to phone so late . . . not sure when we'll be back . . . all very confusing . . . speak up dear . . . something to do with your great grandfather . . . He changed the family name . . . the Light family used to be called the Golightlys . .

A Stormy Night

Poised for action, Ned and Kit stood waiting. But there were no shadows, no familiar swirling mist. In fact, everything was disappointingly normal.

"I suppose we must wait until the house is ready to show us what happened next," said Ned.

The night passed agonizingly slowly and the next day dragged unbearably. Neither felt they could leave the house for fear of missing something, but it was hard to do anything. They tried listening to music, watching television and playing games. They raided the fridge for endless snacks and even Bullseye was restless. At last Kit said what they had both been avoiding.

"Perhaps the haunting has stopped. We know what happened. Shadow time has moved on – Hubble and the letter, and the television scene must have happened months after Thomas Golightly died and Edward was sent away."

But as evening drew on, the house grew strangely hushed and expectant. Darkness fell and the shadows lengthened. An eerie chill crept through the rooms and voices whispered, always just out of earshot. As the mist swirled and their heads reeled, Ned and Kit knew they were once more ghosts from the future in the house of shadows.

They were alone. All was quiet except for the rhythmic tick tock of the clock. Catherine! They knew they had to find her, now, tonight.

"Come on," exclaimed Ned. "We know that Catherine drowned. We must find the lake."

They dashed outside into storm-lashed darkness. Wind howled through the trees and thunder crashed. Only lightning ripping across the sky made it possible to see anything. But where was the lake? As far as Kit knew, there was no lake in their own time. It seemed hopeless, but Ned struggled on. He felt as if he had been there before and knew instinctively which direction to take. Kit followed, battling blindly through wind and rain, desperately hoping Ned was right.

As Kit stumbled through the lashing rain, she realized that they were not the only ones outside on this wild and windy night.

Lakeside Struggle

Ned and Kit hurried on through the trees. They could no longer see either Catherine or Hubble.

"Maybe he's gone the wrong way," yelled Kit, above the noise of the storm. "Perhaps he didn't see Catherine."

Ned was doubtful. "Catherine is in danger. I know it."

Suddenly the lake was in front of them. At first they could see no one. Then Kit gulped in horror. There on a narrow wooden jetty, above the wild, wind tossed water . . .

Was Hubble trying to stop Catherine, or . . .? With a sick feeling in her stomach, Kit knew what would happen next. "She's going to fall and then nothing and no one will be able to save her," she cried. "Come on. We've got to do something!"

But what? They were invisible to the two struggling figures.

"We have to distract Hubble. Remember the letter? He thought he was being haunted," Ned exclaimed, running towards the jetty. "We can use Catherine's cloak."

Kit advanced on Hubble, the cloak billowing in front of her. Ned seized the boat's oar. To Catherine and Hubble it must have looked as if ghostly, unseen hands held the cloak and brandished the oar. Catherine stared in amazement. Hubble looked terrified. He started in horror, backing away from Catherine. Did she realize the "ghosts" were on her side? As Hubble shielded his face, Catherine slipped quickly away through the trees.

Kit flung the cloak over Hubble's head. Ned overturned the boat and threw Catherine's abandoned hat to the waves. To Hubble's eyes, when he finally fought off the cloak, it would look as though Catherine really had drowned.

Graveyard Search

The last thing Kit and Ned saw was Hubble, free at last from the cloak, staring at the upturned boat and bobbing hat. With that, the wind wailed deafeningly. Whirling leaves blurred the scene, then silence. Damp and bedraggled, they were back in their own time.

It was the next morning before Ned and Kit discussed the events of the previous night.

"I still think there is something else," mused Kit. "I don't believe that is the end of the story."

She wandered across to the window and stared out. The figure sitting on one of the broken statues confirmed her feeling. "It's Amos," she yelled, running outside. Ned was close on her heels.

Amos was as elusive as ever. He also seemed to know exactly what had been happening to them.

"I can't stay long," he began. "But you must be prepared. Remember what you have seen and where. Time has passed and Hubble is a haunted man . . . haunted by his own fears, and guilt. His end is near. The date is significant. At the appointed hour, it's up to you."

"What do you mean?" Ned asked. But it was too late. Amos had given his message and as before, in the instant when they glanced away, he had vanished. "Who is he anyway? Is he the Amos we've seen with Catherine and Edward? And how does he know so much?" Ned grumbled.

"Perhaps he's a link between shadow time and our time," Kit muttered. "He said, '. . . his end is near. The date is significant . . .' What date? When did Hubble die?" she paused and then exclaimed, "Maybe the answer is in the graveyard. It's very old. Come on."

The graveyard was quiet and deserted. Enclosed by a moss covered wall, with sheep grazing in the surrounding fields and lit by a bright autumn sun, it was not a bit creepy.

"The oldest graves seem to be over here," said Ned, leading the way. They knew the church was old, but was it old enough? And even if Hubble WAS buried there, his grave might have disappeared long ago.

Sunlight filtered through the trees and there were even some flowers, but the farthest corner was strangely dark and gloomy, as if shrouded in permanent shadow. Kit knew instinctively that was where they should look. Standing a little apart from the rest she found Hubble's gravestone. Was it imagination that made her shiver, or had it grown suddenly colder? Ned pushed aside the long grass and brambles to read the inscription. It was amazingly clear, as if only recently carved.

"Look at the date," he whispered. "It's today."

A Will is Read

Darkness was falling by the time Kit and Ned were home again. Kit blew on her frozen fingers to warm them up. "If the date means anything, something should happen today," she said.

Ned looked dubious. "But what?" he asked. "And what did Amos mean when he said it's up to us?"

It was not long before a familiar mist swirled through the house. The darkness grew blacker and the shadows more dense. With their heads spinning, Ned and Kit found themselves in the house of shadows. Again, a storm raged overhead. Windows rattled and the house shook with each crash of thunder. They were alone in a room. Filled with a sense of urgency that something important was happening, they ventured out into the hall and up the stairs.

Where are we going?

To Hubble's room. I think I know the way.

A low hum of voices came from Hubble's room. Ned opened the door and they slipped silently inside. No one appeared to notice. Kit gulped at the grisly scene in front of her. In the middle of the room, lit by flickering candlelight, propped high on snowy white pillows lay Ebenezer Hubble. A man they had seen before began reading in a solemn voice.

I, Solomon Doolittle, of Doolittle and Dally, now read the last will and testament of Ebenezer Hubble. To my son, Gervase Hubble, I leave my estate and all my worldy goods.

At the lawyer's words, Gervase pulled out a handkerchief and sniffed noisily. "Stop blubbing, boy," growled Hubble from the bed. For a moment Kit felt almost sorry for Gervase.

A blast of cold air and the sound of the door quietly opening and shutting anounced the arrival of someone else.

It was Amos! His piercing eyes looked directly at Kit and Ned as if he could see them. Ned shuffled uneasily. The buzz of voices began to fade until he was only aware of a strange, unnatural silence.

Something was expected of them. Ned's eyes were drawn to the shelves above the desk. A red book – he knew it was Hubble's diary! It held the evidence of his dastardly crime. Solomon Doolittle of Doolittle and Dally must be made to read it.

To the startled group gathered in the room it looked as if a ghostly hand swept the shelf clear. They ducked the flying books which thudded to the floor. One, a bright red volume, landed open in the hands of a shocked looking Solomon Doolittle. He began to read aloud.

All for Nothing

All eyes turned to stare at a horrified Hubble. He gasped and sat bolt upright. "You win after all," he croaked to the air. He pointed to the desk. "All for nothing," he whispered and sank back on the pillows.

Everyone gazed at the desk, but were too shocked to wonder what Hubble was pointing at. Ned knew. Slowly he lifted the lid of the wooden casket.

Only Amos moved. He took out three pieces of paper. Ned and Kit were not surprised to see a small newspaper clipping, the genuine will of Thomas Golightly and a familiar looking letter.

"I knew the will was hidden somewhere, but the letter about Edward is an amazing discovery," Amos spoke so quietly that only Kit and Ned could hear.

They expected the scene to fade at any moment and to find themselves back in their own time. But this was not quite the end.

There was a sudden commotion outside in the hall and a knock at the door. A footman announced the arrival of Lady Golightly-Smarte.

"Who?" Ned glanced at Kit, who looked equally puzzled.

The door opened. All eyes turned expectantly and saw . . . Catherine. She walked slowly into the room, followed by a tall young man. She looked uncertainly at the group gathered around Hubble's bedside.

"What is happening?" she asked. Catherine glanced anxiously at Hubble. "I received a mysterious message telling me to come urgently, and that it was now safe to return."

Amos smiled. With that the scene faded. Ned and Kit found themeselves not in their own time, but outside in brilliant, hot sunshine. They saw Catherine walking with Edward, still weak from his illness. Amos and Henry looked on.

The story seemed finally complete. Kit and Ned had discovered the secret of the old house and righted the ancient crime. They looked back at the house of shadows for the last time.

What Happened Next...

As the outdoor scene faded, their own time solidified around them. Kit and Ned were back inside the house in their own familiar surroundings. Bullseye wagged his tail, pleased to see them. It was two days later when a letter from their parents thudded down onto the doormat.

Hotel Loukanikis
Mythika

September 14th

Dear Kit and Ned,

Hope you are well and not too bored or lonely. We have lots to tell you.

I don't know why they dragged us all the way to Mythika, it seems to be something of a mystery. I told you about your great grandfather changing the family's name - well, it looked as though we had a rather shady ancestor in the distant past that no one knew anything about. As a result, we had been left a few old Mythikan coins and pots. Then suddenly, today, everything changed. A letter had appeared - no one seems to know where from. Mr. Dally could tell us the whole story.

Our ancestor was called Edward Golightly and he only lived on Mythika for a short time. He had been shipwrecked here. He was ill and had lost his memory. The poor boy was only your age Ned, and he didn't have a clue who he was until his sister and her husband eventually rescued him and nursed him back to health at home. Guess what...you'll never believe it, but his estate was Hallows Grange - that old heap we're renting! I know it's a bit of a wreck at the moment and not very big now, but with a little hard work it will soon feel like home.

We'll be back as soon as we can get a flight.

Lots of love,
Mum

Ned and Kit read and reread the letter. Everything seemed to make sense now, including their own link with the Golightly family. But the house held one more surprise.

A strange, new tingling sensation ran down their necks accompanied by a roaring sound that grew louder and louder until it was almost deafening. The ground seemed to shake as dead leaves and papers flew through the air, caught in a sudden whirlwind. Then there was silence and the air was instantly calm.

"What's happening?" whispered Kit. One cautious look told her they were still in their own time. "The house feels different."

Ned and Kit stared at one another. Together, they raced outside as the same incredible idea occurred to them both.

"The house of shadows," Ned gasped.

"As it always was, as if nothing had gone wrong, and the Golightly family had never left," added Kit. "No one could describe it as a 'bit of a wreck' now. What shall we tell Mum and Dad?"

Did You Spot?

You can use this page to help spot things that could be useful in solving the mystery. First, there are hints and clues you can read as you go along. They will give you some idea of what to look out for. Then there are extra notes to read which will tell you more about what happened afterwards.

Hints and Clues

99	What's in a name?
100–101	What do you think the old man's message could mean? Watch out - you might see him again.
102–103	What spooky portraits! Could this be a case for some serious art appreciation?
104–105	Do you recognize the sinister Mr. Hubble? And what about the face framed by the carriage window?
108–109	Do you notice anything strange about the way Ned and Kit look?
110–111	The message on the mirror reads, 'Help' Someone seems to be in trouble, but who?
112–113	Do you notice anything odd at the house? The townspeople are behaving very strangely indeed . . .
114–115	What a mine of information Amos is.
116–117	Do you recognize the man in the portrait? Have you noticed the date?
118–119	Read all the documents carefully.
122–123	Kit and Ned are shortened versions of Catherine and Edward. What about their parents' names? The document Hubble is carrying looks familiar . . .
124–125	Try and sort out the useful from the useless here. Did you know that the Latin word 'fiat' means 'becomes'?
126–127	This man is called Amos and he looks like Amos - could this really be Amos?
128–129	The diary may be important later on.
130-131	Mythika - that's cropped up before. Could there be a connection? Do you recognize Gervase?
134-135	A guilty conscience at work here.
136-137	What could Amos's cryptic message mean?
138-139	Does one of the names Doolittle and Dally ring any bells? Look back right to the beginning of the story.

By the Way . . .

Who was Amos Goodfellow? Was he from the past or present? Perhaps Kit was right when she described him as 'a link between shadow time and our time'- a ghost trying to right an ancient wrong and save his friends the Golightlys from tragedy. After all, Amos mysteriously disappeared once Edward and Catherine were safely home and Hallows Grange was restored to its original size.

Gervase Hubble married Dolores Shrimpton and opened the only kebab restaurant in All Hallows. It was a great success and still exists as the cafe Kit and Ned visited. Gervase, known to his friends as Gerry, has never been happier. He and Dolores had seven children and one of their descendents still runs the cafe today.

Kit in particular was delighted to discover that, along with Hallows Grange, their family had inherited a holiday home in Mythika.

Before Ned's and Kit's involvement in their family history, Edward had continued to live on the island of Mythika, having lost nearly all memory of his previous life. He could only remember his name and the country he came from. Years later, his grandchildren moved away hoping to discover their family's roots. They failed and later changed the family name to Light. After Kit's and Ned's strange adventures in the house of shadows, Edward was quickly pardoned of any crime and returned to his home. He married a girl from Mythika and lived happily in Hallows Grange for the rest of his life.

First published in 1993 by Usborne Publishing Ltd, Usborne House, 83-85 Saffron Hill, London EC1N 8RT, England. Copyright © 1993 Usborne Publishing Ltd. The name Usborne and the device are 🎈 Trade Marks of Usborne Publishing Ltd.

Printed in the UK.   U.E.